TRANQUEB

BENGAL,
The Cold Weather,
1873

Joe Roberts was born in Bath, in the south-west of England, where he still lives. He has travelled widely and written about his travels in three books (*Three-Quarters Of A Footprint, The House of Blue Lights* and *Abdul's Taxi to Kalighat*) and countless newspaper and magazine articles in the United Kingdom, India and the United States. Joe Roberts is also a lecturer in the School of Humanities and Creative Industries at Bath Spa University. He first visited India in 1990 and has returned there as often as possible since. He is married, with three sons. *Bengal, The Cold Weather, 1873* is his first novel.

BENGAL,
The Cold Weather,
1873

A Dream of Edward Lear in India

JOE ROBERTS

TRANQUEBAR

TRANQUEBAR PRESS

An imprint of westland ltd

Venkat Towers, 165, P.H. Road, Maduravoyal, Chennai 600 095

No. 38/10 (New No.5), Raghava Nagar, New Timber Yard Layout, Bangalore 560 026

23/181, Anand Nagar, Nehru Road, Santacruz East, Mumbai 400 055

4322/3, Ansari Road, Daryaganj, New Delhi 110 002

First published in TRANQUEBAR by westland ltd 2012

10 9 8 7 6 5 4 3 2 1

ISBN: 978-93-81626-89-4

Typeset by FourWords Inc.

Printed at Manipal Technologies Ltd., Manipal

Dost thou love picking meat? Or would'st thou see
A man i' th' Clouds, and hear him speak to thee?
Would'st thou be in a Dream, and yet not sleep?

From *Pilgrim's Progress*, John Bunyan

FOREWORD

Edward Lear has been in my thoughts since childhood: the *Books of Nonsense* and the limericks, of course, which I found disappointing. I first came across his landscape paintings as a teenager and from that interest I read Vivien Noakes' *Edward Lear: The Life of a Wanderer.* I have collected books of Lear's drawings, paintings and travels ever since. In the 1980s there was an outstanding television play about Lear called *On the Edge of the Sand.* I read Peter Levi's biography when it came out in the 1990s. I refer to Lear's travels in India in my first Indian book, *Three-Quarters Of A Footprint,* and on that visit I bought *Impossible Picturesqueness: Edward Lear's Indian Watercolours* from Gangaram's in Bangalore. And, of course, there was the major exhibition at the Royal Academy in London.

A few years ago I found a rare volume, *Edward Lear's Indian Journal,* edited by Ray Murphy. I was reading this book in bed, listening to the midnight news on BBC Radio Four, when I fell asleep, sitting up, book in lap. The dream that ensued fascinated me so much that I had to write it down and that sketch became the basis of this book, *Bengal, The Cold Weather, 1873.*

Somehow Lear and his servant Giorgio wandered into a black and white Bengali film, with a strange flickering light, like a worn print of my favourite Satyajit Ray film *Jalsaghar, The*

Music Room, and this too became tangled up with photographs of coal-mining in nineteenth-century Bengal.

There were two things outside the dream that had some effect upon it: the radio, which was still on, became an official British voice and therefore the Raj in my dream, and I had a shooting pain in my feet and ankles that would suddenly attack but not with enough force to wake me so that the pain in the dream would be a sudden shock in the narrative, stepping on a bamboo shoot or an ant's nest, as if the Bengal landscape of paddy-fields and terra cotta temples was full of booby-traps.

When I tried to recreate this dream with its peculiar atmosphere, I had to daydream and reimagine so much. I began to write a Lear of my own imagination, informed by my research but animated in the same way as a fictional character would be. Perhaps there was something more to it than that—I often felt when I was writing that I was really drawing.

Lear's shame about his epilepsy, the demon, was something I could identify with, for as a child I had suffered from *petit mal* seizures, a condition I grew out of, though I still remember the sensations. Occasionally, I get a migraine headache that reminds me of *petit mal*; even though migraines are horrid, they are rather interesting, and they share with epilepsy the weird aura.

I have travelled quite widely over the years in the Indian state of West Bengal and the People's Republic of Bangladesh. I hope my evocation of an undivided Bengal is convincing. Kind Bengali friends have cast an eye over the details of Burrapoker Street.

Bengal, The Cold Weather, 1873 is entirely a work of fiction.

1

A short train journey through verdant countryside, departing after breakfast and arriving by teatime, is surely the most comfortable way to travel. Lear reads Gover's *Folk-Songs of Southern India* and looks out upon palms and thatched barns while Giorgio talks about jackals—there were jackals in Dinapore, wailing at the edges of the garden. He says jackals speak English, and their call is 'Away! Away!' Lear reaches into a bag for his journal.

> *From the verandah, the early morning and brightness of trees is exactly like a lovely autumn, or even June, morning in England; zinnias, balsams and roses included. S– C– in Dinapore said: 'You know, perhaps, that travelling with a European servant is quite exceptional in India.' Mem: No more private houses for either self or servant.*

'Away! Away!' Giorgio repeats it to himself.

'I say, excuse me for butting in but are you talking about shikar?' It turns out the young gent sitting opposite (wearing, Lear observes, striped spats) is on leave from a tea garden, and off to hunt tiger in the Sunderbunds. He talks a great deal about these marshes, to the south-east as the train is headed, then south-east again from Calcutta, some two hundred miles of intersecting creeks and channels, swamps and jungle from the mouth of the Hooghly to the mouth of the Megna. He talks with the ebullience of a schoolboy (he can't be more than twenty-one) but slowly and clearly to Lear and Giorgio, as if addressing deaf people or foreigners. When the poor tigers are exhausted, the young gent starts on cricket but finding this draws no response at all, he asks Lear his line. Lear introduces himself as a landscape painter, his companion as his servant. The young gent is relieved to learn this: he may ignore Giorgio and speak entirely to Lear. 'May I ask where you come from? Your English is very polished.'

In India Lear appears foreign, that is other than British. Something in his manner, his way with handkerchiefs and spectacles. Many of his traits (the uneasiness in society, the refusal to be serious) would seem English enough but Lear remains a puzzle to most of his countrymen.

'I was born in Holloway, but now I live in San Remo...'

He has travelled throughout his life, for the most part outside the Empire. In those wild mountains and deserts Lear is always 'the Englishman', yet among Englishmen he appears foreign.

'But you are, actually, British, not Italian?'

As a young man, Lear claimed Danish origins, with a fanciful ancestor changing the family name from L_r. Now, in his sixties, his style has become Italianate. Britons with whom he is not acquainted might mistake Lear for an Italian opening an hotel somewhere in the mofussil. They would hear him speak Italian to Giorgio. He is taller than most Italians, paler and clumsier: an Italian-Swiss, they might suppose, a bit long in the tooth.

Lear speaks Italian to Giorgio, who is not Italian but an Albanian from Suli, raised in Corfu. Giorgio can also speak Cham, Albanian, Greek, Catering French and large amounts of English in his employer's idiom. Most often, their dialogues range in and out of English and Italian. When Lear speaks English, his voice is high and thin, the yelp of his London childhood still evident. It is not a commanding voice. The

English that Giorgio has learned from Lear sounds querulous and uncomfortable.

Lear tells the young gent he is touring India making preparatory drawings for commissioned oil paintings. It sounds shabby, coming from him, unofficial. Lear feels by nature unofficial, even though some of the oil paintings are commissioned by the highest official there is—Lord Northbrook, the Viceroy of India. Lear carries documents to say as much. They have been close friends for many years. The Viceroy's personal protection should make Lear feel reassured but it doesn't. He senses that people think him too shabby for such august friends, therefore an impostor.

Lear will charm them in the end—he can't help it. Lord Northbrook likes to say Lear has the charm of a child. Lear charms with his wonder and imagination and easy laughter. Nobody sees how precarious it all is, how lonely and unwell the child is. Lear hides his condition scrupulously. Giorgio is invaluable in that respect.

The train rumbles to a halt. They have stopped for no discernible reason in a wood. Lear stands in the carriage and points through the window, 'Look! Painted children!' Three forest boys come through the trees, bare-chested and coated in blue pigment. On their heads they wear conical crowns made of sola pith and they carry bamboo flutes. Lear claps his hands at the young gods. The sight of them walking into the light charms him. The boys come to the window with hands outstretched. The young gent laughs but still feels bound to advise Lear, 'People take them at face value, you see. This one actually is Lord Krishna, and that one is too and so is that one. Took me some time to get to grips with all that, to be honest. Don't give them anything, whatever you do.'

Despite the young gent's warning, Lear produces a tin of peppermint tablets. Thin blue hands with brown palms snatch for the white sweets. With a series of heaves, the train pulls back to life and the boys drop away from the bars of the window. Lear waves until the small blue gods are out of sight, then sits back down mumbling, 'Enchanting...'

'Most of us would call them a nuisance.'

'Not me, then.' Lear folds his arms across his chest. The young gent picks up his paper. Lear picks up his sketchbook. He has a habit of letting his pencil vibrate just above the paper while mustering the drawing in his mind. He scrawls a quick scribble of the three boys. Lear often writes notes around the drawings in his sketchbooks, sometimes deliberately misspelling words in comic phonetic approximations— pharmouse, rox, time and ass-fuddle (thyme and asphodel).

The train reaches Taragunje at four-forty. Lear wishes the young gent good sport, then he and Giorgio step down from their carriage to an unsheltered platform. All around are heaps of coal and, off on a siding, a collection of unhitched and battered wagons, some already occupied by indigent native families. For once, the luggage is gathered without fuss. There is plenty of it. Lear doesn't travel light; besides the trunks he has drawing equipment, stool, easel, telescopes and glasses, and six framed oil paintings wrapped in gunny sack—he's sent the folding rubber bathtub home already. Three porters emerge to carry the baggage to the hotel, their spines quivering like bows under the weight. Lear indicates that the porters should go on ahead. Williams Hotel is advertised as close to the station. He will walk there with Giorgio. They will go slowly, inspecting fruit-stands and shrines. They set off through the bazaar in the slanting light. As they walk, their heavy shoes make clouds of dust. Giorgio looks at the displays of gourds and pitchers while Lear looks up at the trees, still delighted after a month in India by the variety of foliage—the feathery leaves or the leaves that bunch in thick clumps.

A gang of children, distracted from their work of gathering sticks and lumps of coal, follow them. One, the boldest, mimics Giorgio's bow legs, then tugs at the hem of Lear's coat, causing him to spin round and shout boo. Lear buys some oranges—the oranges in India are the sweetest he has tasted, even when the peel is green. An elderly Indian customer who speaks English asks if Lear is staying at the Anthrax Club. 'Williams Hotel,' Lear replies. The oranges are placed in a bag stitched of dried leaves. Lear hands over a few coins then distributes the fruit to the children, who scatter with their booty. The fruit-stand customer exclaims, 'Williams Hotel?'

'I saw it advertised...'

'Such a place, advertised?'

'Why not?'

The old busybody's opinion is not enough to change Lear's mind. He will see for himself if the place is up to scratch.

ဆ 健

The white-robed servants at Williams Hotel are instructed to scrutinise labels: they see that the luggage is bound for Government House. Williams is informed.

A flinty hatchet of a Welshman, born and bred in Bengal, Williams is recovering from a bout of fever that has turned his skin quite yellow.

His bearer Osman Ali comes to dress him. Williams rises from his bed, where he's been sweating for hours under the thinnest of coverlets. Curiosity has given a trembling vigour to his movements. He wrings the cold sweat from his palms. His heart beats like a wing in his chest. Grand personages, at last.

Williams comes to the hall to greet the arrivals. The shutters have to be opened, the tatties rolled up. Smells from the soak-away drain come through. Williams calls the punkahs into service; soon the whitewashed calico fans are flapping air in all directions. Two crouching sweepers, using little splayed brooms, scuttle across the hall floor. A third crouching man follows with a damp rag.

The hotel is a large white building with green gables and shutters and a roof of tin plates and corrugated iron. Lear and Giorgio come up a path lined with white rose bushes in brick-red pots to the portico of the hotel. Williams is proud of his roses, the whitest in the district.

The arrivals are not the dignitaries the hotelier has been led to expect. Williams is not in the habit of smiling at people when he meets them. He finds himself grasping the hands of a dishevelled Englishman he takes to be a teacher of some kind, a tall owlish old creature wearing a dusty black coat slit so high at the back it resembles a beetle's wingcase. A questing nose, more bill than beak; the man's moustache begins up his nose, pours from his nostrils to join his beard. Another older man, possibly Turkish, thinks Williams—not a gentleman. Williams concludes the servants have misread the labels. He looks at Lear, whose grey beard blows here and there under the punkahs, asks no questions but comments on the weather—he warns it may rain in the night. Lear and Giorgio are given two good rooms. They are the only guests in his hotel.

Williams looks at the gaping page beneath the names. There is no denying it has been lean over the winter. In his father's day, Williams Hotel catered to gentlemen in the coal business; men from companies such as Gillander & Arbuthnot took the rooms and conducted business in the hotel. That was before the establishment of the Anthrax Club. As soon as the Club opened, it took the business gentlemen away. It is no doubt more appropriate to conduct coal business in a private environment, among elected members of the same industry. The dormitory wing at the Anthrax Club is no doubt more comfortable.

A few years ago, Williams applied for membership. He would have thought, as a British businessman in the Taragunje coalfields, he would make a suitable member but his application was rejected. At the time it had smarted, but it did not occur to Williams that the decision was based upon the swarthiness of his wife and children. Williams put it down to people finding his shortage of names (only two and those the same) off-putting.

Without the coal managers, Williams Hotel has relied on railway passengers and, over the years, trade has been steady enough. Within the last month, however, business has come to a standstill. He suspects there are reasons for this. Passengers could be using the newly repainted retiring rooms at the station itself. What's more, the train times have changed. It is possible to come in from Howrah in a sleeping carriage, attend one's business in Taragunje and at day's end head back to Calcutta in another—no need for a room at all.

In his room on the floor above, Lear undresses to bathe. On the wall beside the press there is a text in an Oxford frame. Lear knows these things from religious households, but it is an unusual one. All in a mock-Elizabethan script with loops hanging from almost every word. The first three lines are in a language Lear takes to be Welsh. The next three lines offer an English translation:

> The white martyrdom is exile.
> The green martyrdom is penitence.
> The red martyrdom is sacrifice.

In the corner of the cream mount, an incompetent sketch of a monk or a saint feeding animals. Lear cannot abide monks. He went to Athos once; vile place, such silliness, old men muttering, the unnecessariness of it all.

Looking in the long glass, Lear can't believe he has become so old—there hardly seems to have been the time to grow so old. Sixty-one. He finds his own appearance absurd: the discrepancy between his physique (lumbering) and his manner (timid). Lear has learned to bear his lack of beauty; he no longer seeks physical love. Through his sensibility and charm, he is sought after as a friend. Still, he would rather have the deeper involvements of loving another and being loved. His sister had loved him, of that he is certain, but not his parents.

When he takes his bath, he is disheartened by the clumsiness of his body. A wounded octopus. He sometimes draws himself in letters to friends, emphasising the globularity of his torso and the inadequacy of his legs. In these drawings his spectacles are always springing from his nose and sometimes he draws them with pupils like a second pair of eyes. In one drawing he sits, with his arms flung out behind him, on the shoulders of a runaway elephant.

At six Osman Ali comes to Williams' room. They speak together in Urdu. Osman Ali informs Williams that Lear is an English landscape painter resident in Italy. 'Painter?' The hotelier's nose twitches. Osman Ali says the other man is Lear's servant.

'Is the servant a Turk?' asks Williams.

'He is not a Mussulman,' declares Osman Ali with mysterious certainty.

'That surprises me. I'd taken him for a Turk.'

'Maybe Italian, Sahib.'

Williams finds Lear at the piano, playing comical waltzes for the children. Williams encourages his children to chatter with the guests. His son speaks clearly without the native lilt, but his daughter speaks singsong English. Lear asks their names.

The girl sings Patience Williams. The boy says William Williams. Lear remarks it is quite Welsh to have the name twice.

'He is named after myself, Welsh and proud to be so,' declares Williams Senior. 'I am the son of William Williams, the grandson of William Williams. We are links in a mighty chain.'

He resembles a bird, thinks Lear. The downward jabbing movement of his head while the round eye rolls up to keep your gaze. As for the double names: Lear remarks that there is no apostrophe in the hotel's name; were there to be one, would it come before or after the s? There would be a degree of intimacy in it. In other words, does he keep his hotel as William, as in Chez Guillaume, or as Mr Williams, more usual in Wales and the rest of the Empire?

Williams thinks for a moment and replies: 'There is no need. I am Williams, my establishment has my name on it. Just as my shirt has my name on its collar.'

'Father says I am William Williams the tenth.'

'That is a charming impression of Mount Snowdon in my room.'

'How clever of you to recognise Snowdon.'

'Mountains are good business, Mr Williams...'

'My father was born at the Griffin Llanberis,' says Williams, 'as was my grandfather, as was my great...' The gent's lying, thinks Lear, he's East Indian, Eurasian: no Welshman is that colour. Williams, as if hearing Lear's misgivings, says, 'Both Father and Mother's families were listed in the *Anglesey and Caernavonshire Families*, Mr Lear.'

The boy pipes in again, 'Father has added our names to the book.'

'I say,' says Lear, impressed.

'He writes a fine medieval hand...'

Williams shouts at his son, 'Do not be ironical with me!'

The children are sent out. They leave reluctantly; merriment is rare enough in the hotel. Lear pines for all banished children.

The earliest of all the morbidnesses I can recollect must have been somewhere about 1819—when my Father took me to a field near Highgate, where there was a rural performance of gymnastic clowns &c.—& a band. The music was good—at least it attracted me: the sunset & twilight I remember as if yesterday. And I can recollect crying half the night after all the small gaiety broke up—& also suffering for days at the memory of the past scene.

Williams rises from his chair and walks forward with a low bow for several paces before straightening up. Lear is invited to the family table. There he is introduced to Mrs Williams, who is quite dark, draped in festive tartan. She wears her hair in a long plait decorated with hibiscus flowers. Mrs Williams smiles in a bored way, as if yawning without opening her mouth at all. The small chandelier, a rackety thing with cups of red glass, throws patches of pink light about the room.

They start the meal with a thin soup, the water from boiling a chicken augmented with curry powder. The entrée, Williams tells Lear, is Taragunje Stew, a dish of his father's devising. It has to be prepared at the table by the host, using a silver pan (no other metal will do, he says) and a chafing lamp. The soup plates are taken, then the servants bring in the stew apparatus: the stove with its blue flame and the silver pan. The silver is whiter than English silver and much softer. A servant brings in a steaming cauldron. It is the soup again. Into the pan, Williams ladles two helpings of the soup, then pieces of boiled fowl, a bowlful of mashed anchovies, all brought in succession from the kitchen, roasted onions (the small Indian variety), a jar of pickled oysters, some cayenne pepper and a squeeze of lime. Finally, into the stew goes a glass of Madeira.

'Taragunje Stew,' says Williams, stirring the mixture until it bubbles. It is served upon a mound of rice. Williams advises Lear that his wife speaks little English. 'She has no curiosity to learn,' he says gravely. Neither has she curiosity to eat, Lear observes, and nor has Williams who takes little of his stew—an unhappy dish, Lear finds—the flavours don't merge at all—the oysters taste not of the sea but of brine and ammonia.

'Can you grow watercresses in Bengal?'

Many years ago in Albania, Lear tells them, he found some capital cress in a little stream. The local people did not eat the stuff, so when Lear started to eat the cress with some bread and cheese he had in his bag, he provoked much curiosity and laughter. The foreigner was eating weeds! What else might he eat? One brought a thistle for him, another a stick, a third some grass and a fourth a grasshopper.

It is supposed to be a funny story but neither Williams nor his wife laugh. Lear sees they may think he is criticising the thrown-together nature of Taragunje Stew. They all drink Madeira. Mrs Williams takes this by the bumper, sipping through puckered lips as if kissing the rim of her glass, remaining silent through the meal.

A place at a separate table has been laid for Giorgio, who comes in slightly late for the soup. He is not offered wine nor is he invited to share the stew, though there is plenty left for him, but is served cold mutton instead. The salt on the table is moist and grey. He tastes a pinch. It tastes of the sea. He crumbles some salt on the meat—it brings out a flavour that makes him homesick. The meat is tough in India, the water tastes soapy. Lear turns around in his chair to ask, '*Ti piace* the mutton, Giorgio?'

Giorgio is fifty-one, ten years younger than Lear but his weather-beaten skin and white hair make him look the older man; Lear's skin remains as pink as a boy's beneath his whiskers. Giorgio's boxy Albanian skull and jutting white whiskers give him a rat-catcher terrier's head. Lear does not like dogs but he has found Giorgio's ferocious appearance useful on occasion. They have been together a long time. It is not always plain sailing. Giorgio can be critical at times. He knows Lear's sensitivities and manipulates them. If Lear catches him doing this, he sulks.

Between chews, Giorgio answers: 'Is like chewing a belt.'

Lear knows that Giorgio is as disappointed in the food as he is disappointed in India. It is too starchy for him. He expected something different: not sandwiches and silver bands but souks and brigands. He honestly believes they are in India to become rich, despite all Lear tells him; he still expects to go home with chests of gold coins, tusks of ivory.

Williams tells Lear that an artist has drawn his likeness recently, while he was sleeping in his chair. The artist stayed one night, earlier in the cool weather. He left without settling his bill. 'It is not a flattering picture. I think he left it to spite me. He depicts me as a lazy man,' says Williams. 'The truth is I am often debilitated. By illness, Mr Lear, flux. My bowels...'

'May I see the drawing?'

'You may not. I do not show it to my guests.'

'Why don't you burn it?'

'The drawing is signed. It may be used in a court of law, if necessary.'

As Lear leaves the dining-room, Williams advises him again that it may rain in the night. Lear, knowing that rain at this time of year is not to be expected, is surprised. Williams explains, 'Our seasons here—each one is so distinct from the other. It feels as if each is a different country—the garden changes, different flowers and flowering trees. There may be rain in the cold weather months, just are there may be clear days during the monsoon. And in late spring, there are the mango rains. My gardener Banamali is something of a weather-prophet. He told my bearer it will rain in the night. I have never known him to be wrong.'

Osman Ali approaches Lear in the hall. 'Do you have books, Master? Do you like stories?' He is holding a small pile of notebooks, leather-bound, perhaps somebody's diaries.

'Where did you get those?'

Osman Ali holds one open: the pages hand-written some time ago, brown ink on onion paper, in close script. Beside the writing, in the margins, there are scrawled figures in lewd attitudes. 'Exciting stories, Sahib.'

'I don't need excitement. Good night to you.'

Lear has corns on the little toes of both feet. His toes splay and his boots pinch. Lying down, if he crosses his legs just above the ankle, and then positions his feet anklebone to anklebone, he can press the corns together. This creates an odd sensation, as if an electric wave is passing up his shins. The jolt doesn't reach his knees, which he suspects are made of coral.

Downstairs, alone, Williams feels his scalp prickle, a trickle of sweat behind his ear; the fever has returned. He goes back to his bedroom and lies down without undressing. The sheets have been changed, a fresh coverlet lain. His teeth rattle a tarantella, through which he can hear his breath, pitched at a high squeal. The punkah goes back and forth. He fancies the squeal is forming words in Bengali. Williams is adamant that the words of his breath are not his thoughts. He speaks several Indian languages but he's certain that he thinks in English—he does remember his father professing to speak in English but think in Welsh.

To prove that the words are not his thoughts, Williams sets about translating them into English. This distresses him, for the high-pitched voice is slandering and malicious, delivering dark allegations about his reputation in coarse language. He sits up and holds his jaw clamped with both hands to stop it. He blames his wife. If she were beside him she might distract him from such harmful self-absorption. Mrs Williams never speaks. Williams talks to her and her eyes respond. For all their years together, it has been enough. His wife is a fine and capable woman; he senses the pattern of her tastes and dislikes, he knows how to amuse her and when to leave her alone. Williams still finds his wife mysterious. Now the teeth are gibbering in English: 'Now. What a curious word, now. Now then. Odd. Put together like that. Where will it lead you? Do you agree? You can't really say it, can you? Now. Because it's not quick enough. By the time you've said Now, it's over. It's not that Now anymore, it's this Now...' It is seven months since they've shared the room; she sleeps elsewhere. He stirs two large dashes of Propter's Panacea into a beaker of water. It is a restorative tonic he takes; among its ingredients is Datura Stramonium. 'Efficacious for Neuralgia,

Headaches, Biliousness, Constipation, Indigestion, Dizziness, Torpid Liver...'

ဆ ဆ

At around three in the morning Lear wakes with a start. There are two angry hornets, long and black and noisy, in his room. They bang into the walls and even the headboard of his bed—there is no mosquito net to protect him. Lear sits up in his nightshirt, terrified they will sting him. He calls out for Giorgio but remembers that he is sleeping on the ground floor. He goes to the door and shouts for assistance. He expects Osman Ali to appear but instead Williams arrives, still dressed. 'May I help you?' he asks Lear.

'There are two, um, creatures in here...'

'Creatures?'

'Hornets, I think. They look even fiercer than the Italian ones.'

'That's because it is going to rain. You didn't close the window.'

The only thing that matters to Lear is removing the insects from his room. 'It is not difficult,' says Williams, pushing past him. Beside the bed, there is a bell-metal beaker that Williams takes. One hornet has settled on the wall, buzzing and flexing in a punch-drunk manner. Williams places the beaker over the hornet which, trapped, makes a terrible ringing sound against the sides of the vessel. 'If you would hand me that pad for a moment?' Williams slides the pad under the beaker, walks to the window and releases the first hornet into the night. Osman Ali suddenly appears, grinning foolishly. Williams shouts something at him in a native language and Osman Ali starts to wave his arms. 'No, no,' says Williams in English, 'gently, gently'. He hands Osman Ali the beaker. Osman Ali does not understand what to do. As the remaining hornet settles on the arm of a chair, he simply tries to bash it with the beaker. He misses and the enraged creature flies about in a frenzy. It lands in Lear's beard. Lear looks about to faint. Williams tugs at the beard and the hornet stings him on the back of his hand. 'Hoy! Hoy! Hoy!' he calls out, his yellow face darkening in pain. The hornet, meanwhile, is still at large. Osman Ali swings a hand-towel at it. Williams crouches on the bed. Eventually, after a minute or so, the servant brings it down. He has no shoes on so Williams stamps upon it. Osman Ali picks up the crushed form and puts it in Lear's chamber-pot. Poor Williams' hand is already swelling. Lear is concerned for him. He holds the hotelier's hand in his own. The two men look into each other's eyes. Lear pats the wrist of the wounded hand. For a second or two, Williams feels as cherished as a small baby—it is a strange feeling, causing some bashfulness. His eyes slide away from Lear's. 'Don't worry. Don't worry about me,' he mutters, overcome by Lear's gesture, 'I shall treat it with baking powder'.

'Will that work?'

'Oh, I should think so,' says Williams, then, as if speaking to himself, he adds wistfully, 'What is a little pain?' The two men leave Lear's room. It does rain as Williams' gardener had predicted, feeble unseasonal rain that patters on the tin roof.

When Lear gets back to sleep, it is a shallow sleep that brings with it no refreshment. He can hear his sister Ann (dead some twelve years, to his grief) telling him to be careful, her soft voice reading to him. The twentieth of twenty-one children, Lear was raised mostly by Ann, who was twenty-two years older; Ann took him over when his mother became exhausted. She raised her young brother as if he were her son, she gave her life to him. Ann wasn't pretty any more than Lear is handsome, indeed she had a beardless version of his face, but her goodness was evident in her eyes and the symmetry of her bonnet around her face and the shy serenity of her smile. Lear remembers living in her kindly shadow, in rooms that were painted with gravy; Ann watching him fall asleep: 'Lie still, and have no fear.' If he scratched or fidgeted in the night, her voice floated through the dark telling him not to provoke the demon. Lear would conjure up visions, airy bodies, made up of feathers and leaves. These bodies would rise at the foot of the bed, from the right-hand corner and move slowly by in a semi-circle to disappear on his left—the shapes of birds and butterflies, of upright cats in suits of clothes, of plants, trees, musical instruments, harpists and flautists, but neither voice nor sound was heard. Ann urged him to recreate these imaginings. She would find feathers and flowers for him to draw. When Ann was despondent or disappointed she read aloud from books of morbid verse; her voice would twitter like the cold murmur of a London breeze. Lear feels remorse at some failure or betrayal, too general to be tied to any particular incident, a feeling of letting Ann down.

We live & live & live, & live on & perhaps so living from day to day through these long years, feel these losses less—' There are subterranean disturbances as well, angers which might come to face you like stern beings who would wrest confessions...'

Lear is soured in his chest, swamped with gastric acid from the Taragunje Stew. He sits up gasping like a fish. There is a bell-metal water-jug beside his bed (Lear has seen these in the market) and a posy of sweet peas. These consoling touches suggest the country-bred influence of Mrs Williams; in themselves enough to divert Lear from the black imps and the scorpious snakes and the other horrors that stalk his dreams. In late middle age (early old age) Lear is still mortified by shameful events of his childhood. The memories dog him, they lollop up when he least expects them, panting their damp breath in his ears and licking him around the mouth.

At five, he is woken again by a banging on the door. 'Who is it?' Lear shouts.

'Pishpot dumpy,' comes the reply (it is a servant, but not Osman Ali).

'No, thank you,' mumbles Lear; there is only the dead hornet in it, not worth the disturbance. He hears the man clear his throat as he stumps away again.

೮ ೮

Throughout the first weeks Lear draws with speed, his hand whirring over the paper. The December weather is good for plein-air. Giorgio compares it to the spring in Corfu. Lear knows to make the most of it, even though he hasn't suffered the intolerable heat yet nor the monsoon that will drive him indoors for months. To achieve as much plein-air work as possible, Lear rises early.

'Let us advance into the healthful air...'

He sets out with Giorgio from the hotel at six. Giorgio is pleased to have had a comfortable room.

In Dinapore, Giorgio slept in the servants' quarters, with a drunken cook who told him in English that he was the first European servant he had set eyes on. He kept saying, 'Your skin is darker than mine.' In the night the cook made improper advances. Giorgio knocked his teeth out.

Lear did not tell his host. S– C– knew that his cook was bibulous and put the smashed teeth down to drunken misadventure. Nevertheless, Lear worries the cook, all be he bibulous, was acting upon the general misapprehension that S– C– suggested. Enough.

Lear: 'And what do you make of our host Mr Williams, Giorgio?'

Giorgio: 'He is an impostor, he pretends to be English...'

'He claims, in fact, to be Welsh...'

'What is Welsh?'

'*Il Galles. Mi dice che sia Gallese.*'

'His skin is the wrong colour.'

'He is a strange colour, I must say. I think that is due to illness.'

'What is this illness? *Febbre gialla?*'

A smoky mist hangs in the air. It smells to Lear of dying fires and cinnamon. They walk beside the scruffy encampments along the tracks. The town of Taragunje, such as it is, consists mainly of coal-heaps and goods-yards. The first stirrings of the day: rising figures casting off grey shawls, yellow dogs stretching. Turning a corner, they see a thin coughing sweeper carrying a tray of night-soil on his head, a stinking Quangle-Wangle's hat decorated with blue flies. Hundreds of little black wagtails fidget along the telegraph wires behind him, alert to the blue flies.

They reach the station, then set off over scarred fields that stretch away under the morning sun. Giorgio declares, 'I think this was a battlefield, long time ago, *nei periodi antichi...*'

Lear replies wrily, 'All flesh is grass, Giorgio.'

They walk with their heads down, to check each footing, towards a colossal banyan tree, the biggest Lear has seen, like a great green circus tent.

Lear asks, 'Giorgio, have you ever seen a tree *questo grande*?'

Giorgio, who often thinks in terms of composition, replies, 'Is the wrong shape, *troppo grande...*' He means it would fill a picture with green and brown. They step cautiously inside. The central trunk has thrown out many branches that have themselves become trunks. The whole thing seems to Lear more architecture than nature. Inside the green tent, it is dark and still. '*Piano,*' Giorgio hisses.

They are not alone. Someone is sleeping among the trunks, curled under a sunset-coloured cloth in a nest of leaves. A large man with bells around his ankles. Beside the sleeper are a drum and a zither, a scroll tied with yellow ribbon, a row of small baskets and a painted clay figure.

Lear and Giorgio tiptoe out and say nothing until they are a long way off. Then Giorgio clears his throat, hawks and spits through his moustaches. '*Zingaro.*'

The walk back—camels and coolies, oxen and drivers, goats and some queerly-behaved light-grey jays (he has seen the birds at Lucknow but does not know their name).

Returning to Williams Hotel, they notice the roses have disappeared from the potted bushes. Williams, who wears a white gauze bandage on his stung hand, is frantic. 'Blasted monkeys! Ate the lot in half an hour. It happened last winter as well. My early roses. It's because they're so white. I'll bet they taste like milk to the brutes.'

At breakfast, Lear tells Williams about the sleeping gipsy. 'There is a market at that garden every Tuesday,' explains Williams, still fuming, 'nobody's likely to be sleeping'.

Lear says there was no market, just a sleeping gipsy—they must be talking about different gardens. 'A big chap too, fast asleep under the great banyan.'

Silence. Then, 'Oh, I doubt it,' says Williams—a trifle sharply, thinks Lear.

After fifteen minutes of scowling, Williams does show the drawing, just as Lear had been expecting him to. He suspects the hotelier is secretly proud of his portrait. It is quite harmless: a study of a man asleep in a chair with his chin in his chest. 'It suggests dissipation,' says Williams, 'but I am weakened only by my bowels...'

'I know Slingsby Moore,' mutters Lear, patting his mouth with a napkin. He could put a face to the signature, if not the drawing. He finds the line scratchy. He recalls Slingsby Moore, round and smudgy, companionable. In his cups, he would reveal secrets: that his Mama called him Pooh, that his real name isn't Moore at all but something like Mormenides, his father being a Jew from Chios. There had been murmurings of debt. His presence in India is a surprise to Lear, but not a worry. Moore, in his opinion, is no rival. An unfortunate fellow, if anything at all, who might ask to borrow money.

'The same Slingsby Moore?' asks Williams.

'Yes. Not well. Don't vex yourself. He doesn't suggest anything but a hard-working gent at rest. It's pleasant.'

Again Williams is touched by the older man's kindness. The feeling embarrasses him so he just huffs and leaves the table, holding his bandaged hand before him like a collie-dog with a wounded paw.

Back in his room, drawing with his pen on a tablet of cartridge paper, Lear can hear a man singing softly in the garden. He cannot understand the words but the hymn-like melody, sad and reflective, draws him in. He listens transfixed, though there may be a little flutter of wings against the sun or the faint tapping of a branch against the gable (where the weight of some small bird makes it move) to distract him. A cloud covers the sun and the room darkens, stilling Lear's thoughts; the calm religious song holds him in its green depths. He is aware only of his ears straining to hear each note.

The boy William shows Lear around the hotel garden. He is a solemn child. Lear says to him, 'I shall call you Billy.'

William replies, 'Please don't. It sounds like a cat.'

Patience walks a few shy steps behind them. Lear tells the children, 'I have a cat called Aderphos. I call him Foss. I had his twin first, Potiphar, but he died.'

The garden is really a mango orchard, or tope as it's called, with tubs of bright flowers—some unknown to Lear, with thickish stems and disproportionately small blue or mauve flowers—interspersed among the trees and white wrought-iron seats with scarlet cushions.

'And do you sit and eat the mangos here?'

The children nod. 'Oh yes, but the season is very short.'

'This is the gardener Banamali,' says William as a tall meek old man (dressed in a kind of toga) comes forward with an orange flower for Lear's button-hole. Banamali means 'gardener of the forest'. The hymn-singer, Lear surmises. Old Banamali is a Santal whose village is surrounded by forest. Banamali is a name that is sometimes given to Lord Krishna as well, in his case because the Hindus believe he causes all the trees to blossom and bear fruit. William trails off cautiously with this information, looking up at Lear.

Banamali understands English but does not speak to the guests. He could explain that Santals are not Hindus, they have their own complicated religion, with personal gods, family gods, village gods and more general gods, but in the trees behind Lear he can see, to his consternation, a troop of monkeys: the old Gora-Sahib must have brought them with him.

A few moments later, they hear two shots from a rifle. Williams misses the monkeys who dance away through the branches.

Lear stands very still—in those seconds the approach of death, stopping just this side of annihilation: a suspended net of confusion, dissolution without re-creation, where this world and other worlds interpenetrate—while the two children clutch his hands, as if to reassure themselves he has not died of fright. From the touch of their fingers, Lear regains himself.

'Be gone!' Williams Senior shouts at the trees. 'Vandals! Fornicators! Philistines!'

To Lear, he explains: 'I can't shoot straight with this on my hand...'

As Patience skips back to the verandah, the boy William looks at Lear and says coldly: 'I don't like my father much.'

'I'm sure he's a nice man really. Monkeys can be vexing, especially to gardeners...'

The boy shakes his head. 'It's nothing to do with monkeys. He smells so. I don't think British men should smell like that.'

'I haven't noticed a smell. What does your mother say?'

The boy just raises his eyebrows and shrugs.

'What does he smell of?'

'He smells of mould. The way a blanket smells if it's left in the damp.'

'How curious,' remarks Lear, who feared and yearned for his own father; he can remember shuddering at the bristles on his father's cheek, the yellowness of his teeth, the smell of his breath like wet fallen leaves.

William says, 'Yes, it is. If he comes close to me, I don't breathe. It's hard to explain. I don't want to be like that when I'm grown up. I don't want to breathe the same dust...'

'Would you like to keep a hotel?'

'It would be the worst thing imaginable.'

'Do you want to live in India?'

'Absolutely not,' declares William.

'Where would you live?'

'Paris, I should think.'

'Have you been there?'

'I haven't been anywhere except here.'

'You must learn to speak French.'

'That is why I have asked Papa to send me to school in Chandernagore.'

'And how shall you live in Paris when you get there, William?'

'Perhaps I'll write some books...'

'Oho,' Lear tilts his head, 'about?'

The boy retreats at the question, as a snail pulls in its horns. His daydreams are not usually taken seriously. The truth is the books he would write keep changing. To change the subject the boy resumes his role as garden-guide: 'Have you ever seen a handkerchief tree?'

And Lear (to show that he is fully himself again—out of the net of confusion) bursts into *The Banks O' Doon*, his own version of Burns' song, which he trills in an emotional Highland brogue:

> 'Ye banks and braes o' bonny Doon,
> How can ye bloom sae fresh and fair;
> How can ye chant, ye little birds,
> And I sae feary, fu o'care!
> Thou'll break my heart, thou warbling bird,
> That wantons through the flowering thorn:
> Thou minds me o' departed joys.
> Departed—never to return...'

2

---

*I*n a loud voice, as if reciting to the passing river-bank, the man in the cabin declaims: 'Then hand in hand by the edge of the sand, they danced by the light of the moon, the moon, the moon...' He can't tell how serious these poems are. He presumes they are serious. Funny but serious, with birds flying away never to return and people (often deformed) leaving on perilous voyages.

Raja Pannalal Chandranath Dey of Barapukur is travelling from his country estate to join his wife in Calcutta.

The first part of this journey is easiest by boat.

Dey feels listless but comfortable, sitting in his tiny cabin, looking at himself in a hand-glass: sleek, smooth-jowled, a man of fifty. Light-skinned, with green shadows under green eyes—green eyes are common in his family, to do with iron in mustard leaves. The eyes bulge, and the grains of both tear-ducts are stained red. When he opens his mouth, his gums and tongue are red as well. His lips are black. His hair is black and brushed into neat oiled strands. Dey leaves his cabin to read on the deck. The river, one of the many tributaries that thread the delta, has no current to speak of and the sedge on its banks is undisturbed by wind.

The boat, built in Dacca for his grandfather eighty years ago, is a keelless barge called a budgerow, painted in red, white and green. Two-thirds of its length is taken up by cabins, with jilmils like Venetian slats. Above the cabins, on their roof, is a furled sail. The other third of the boat is occupied by a dozen oarsmen standing in pairs. They have been ordered not to sing.

The cabins are occupied by Dey and a few of the scholarly retainers he is taking from Bhavani to work in the Burrapoker Street libraries. Everyone reads quietly. Dey sits in a basket chair on the roof, wearing a long embroidered shawl against the breeze. He is still, thoughtful and silent, reading the English book from Thacker & Spink. The book is bound in green calf. The pictures are in a style that reminds Dey of the woodcut printers in the bazaars around Burrapoker Street. He can see the cruel British humour in them. He finds the poems disturbing rather than amusing. The book was recommended by his cousin Jagadish who finds the poems hilarious. Dey senses morbidity and fidgetiness in them, even despair. Very little to laugh at.

After an hour, they pass some boats moored in a row. Dey looks up from his book. On the upper deck of one a boatman is asleep, rolled like a cigar in a brown sheet from head to toe. On another, a man twists some yarn into rope. On the lower deck an old bare-chested man stares back at Dey with an expression of accusation. On land the people amble slowly, as if without purpose. Some sit at the water's edge or rest on their haunches embracing their knees. Dey remarks how still it all is.

The boat leaves the sluggish little river, dropping down into the current of a brisker stream where the water loses its coating of slime and spreads out into a marsh. Here and there islands of grass rise from the water in which the sky is reflected: the islands become green clouds floating through air. Dey leaves the upper deck to sit below. The waters of the marsh find an outlet in a winding channel only seven yards wide, through which they rush swiftly, the box-like budgerow in a sudden violent struggle. The current hurls the clumsy craft along at breakneck speed and the crew use their oars as poles to prevent it being dashed against the banks. The scholars topple about. Dey and the boatmen laugh and cheer as they are delivered into the open river. By noon, a damp wind blows, carrying flickers of rain like news from downriver. The crew all shiver. Dey's mood sinks. At two in the afternoon the sun comes out again. The banks are now high and covered with peaceful groves. Where the boat is moored that evening, the bamboo poles of fishermen are planted. Kites hover above the nets. At the water's edge paddy birds stand in meditation, all kinds of waterfowl. The boatmen cook their rice. Dey puts the poetry book aside.

Looking out over the river, he sees an ungainly bird splashing, attempting to scramble through the reeds to the bank. It is a hen that has escaped the galley. An oarsman wades out and wrings the fowl's neck. Everybody laughs. Dey orders the cook not to serve him that chicken. Feed it to the boatmen instead. He and his assistants will take fish and bitter greens. He craves bitterness in his food: bitter gourd, neem leaves. There is the sound of a drum, beating like a pulse, and the sound of ankle-bells. Dey is told that the minstrel Hathi Das Baul is under the longan tree.

'Bring him, bring him...'

The villagers say when Hathi Das Baul dances and stamps his feet, the ground shakes. When he sings, his voice is as loud as a trumpet; pots sometimes crack. When he dances, he spins like a dervish. His preaching borrows as much from the dervishes in Dacca as from the Bhakti saints the villagers revere. The villagers don't know the Baul's real name. They don't know his original caste; he could even be a Mussulman. Their own faith is expressed through devotion, so they are moved by the Baul's ecstatic songs. The words are twilight-language, all symbols, everything means something else but the villagers hear the meaning in the blaring music of Hathi's voice. They know the words are about God: Hathi Das sings about the pain of separation in a song about guava trees, about the ecstasy of communion in a song about rowing boats. The villagers have been told that God comes to the thought of those who know him beyond thought, not to those who imagine he may be summoned by thinking. God may be unknown to the learned and known to the simple.

Hathi wears a patchwork shawl of orange, pink and red over a loose crimson robe and orange pajamas, the bright colours singing out from the green shade. He unties his orange puggaree and combs his long hair. He has no beard, just a few long catfish whiskers about his lower lip. Around his ankles he wears strings of bells; bells in the shape of rosebuds. His instruments are beside him, the single-stringed gopiyantra, the small hand drum. He doesn't need much, he is within a day's walk from home. He is listening to the voices of people and livestock. The sun is about to sink and the air smells of dung and sugarcane. He's made a small fire, for warmth not for cooking. He takes great care not to be seen eating. He is not at all emaciated, he's as broad as a door. He is called Hathi, which means 'elephant', because of his size; he's almost a giant. Hathi packs his chillum, lights it with a twig, inhales the smoke through cupped hands. He sits back against the tree, stupefied for a moment. Then his eyes blaze red. Smoke flares from his nostrils. A stranger, a messenger, approaches from the ghat.

The giant Baul bows before the Raja and his scholars. Hathi Das Baul knows something of Dey: the Raja is said to be absent-minded by his servants, as lost as an opium addict in the world of his thoughts. It seems the Raja is puzzled by a riddle. The riddle is written down in an Englishman's book, decorated with squiggly drawings. An owl and a cat go to sea in a boat made of leaves. The owl feels desire for the cat. He serenades her, playing a veena. The cat is charmed by the owl's singing. They agree to marry and sail to an island where bhang is produced. A pig brings them a golden ring.

An English peacock performs the ritual. They partake of keema and English mangoes, and then they dance on the sea strand.

Days later, when Hathi tells his wife of the encounter, she asks him: 'Is that all? Was there no child of this marriage? What did you say to him?'

Hathi rocks with laughter. 'I told him the elephant drinks blood and milk, blood and milk. The sun goes down in a lake of pearls...'

She covers her mouth with amusement. 'You said that to the Raja?'

'He paid me ten rupees.'

In the night, Hathi's wife shakes him awake. 'A bat!'

'What about a bat?'

'The child of an owl and a cat...'

'The Raja was not asking about their child.'

Dey takes the book back to the chair on the roof of the cabins, to read beside the lantern. When he has finished reading, the lantern splutters, it is late at night. His eyes are smarting. He puts out the lamp and sits in the dark, listening to the waves that, driven by the wind, slap constantly against the stern. The distant village sleeps, nestling behind a fringe of trees. From the bank comes the sustained chirrup of crickets.

In the last century, Tilly Kettle had painted a fine portrait of Dey's ancestor, Raja Matilal Chandranath Dey of Barapukur. The Raja stands beneath a Mughal arch, with one hand outstretched to the viewer; he looks plump in a quilted, sashed coat and a fur-rimmed hat. His face is puffy and he has a large waxed moustache. Matilal would have been thirty at the time but he looks much older, nearer fifty. The painting was the first acquisition in the Dey family's collection of European art. No member of the family has ever travelled beyond India; the paintings (often pieces of questionable attribution) are presents from business acquaintances or bought at auction-houses. This is not because the Deys lack discernment but because for years they have had to rely on London agents only too happy to acquire the unsold pictures of West End galleries. All three of their palaces are filled with huge dark oil paintings of varying quality, some almost entirely black. There are marble statues, ordered from Italian catalogues, and bulbous Chinese vases. Landscape paintings are Dey's favourites: rarely Indian, more often of rural England, Mediterranean vistas or the Holy Land.

Lear's large work, *Philae at Sunset*, Dey loves for its ruins, palms and reflections, without knowing where Philae is. This painting hangs at Bhavani Place. It is the finest painting the family have acquired in the century since the Kettle portrait.

A Scotsman gave Dey two volumes, *The Journals of a Landscape Painter in Greece and Albania* and *The Journals of a Landscape Painter in Southern Calabria and the Kingdom of Naples*, explaining that the books are the work of the same artist who'd painted the ruins. This Scot, a planter of indigo, considers Lear no more than a petit maitre. The phrase means nothing to Dey. Little by little, he learns more of the painter. He discovers that Lear has given Queen Victoria drawing lessons. Word comes to him that Lear is a friend of the Viceroy. He knows that Lear is a royal name in England; he has seen Shakespeare's play performed, by English players not Indians. Dey acquires another book by Lear—this one from Thacker & Spink, called *Nonsense Songs, Stories, Botany and Alphabets*.

The boat reaches a jetty. Dey disembarks, accompanied by the scholars and other attendants. The party take their positions in two chartered tongas. The splintery carts clatter along the red kutcha tracks in the direction of the railway station. The second stage of the journey to Calcutta is easiest by rail.

3

The mites that dance and tumble across one's vision are not flecks of dust on the eyeball. They're not on the eye at all but in the liver; impurities in the liver. Less explicable (from experience, more sinister) to Lear is the sparkler that for days now has occupied the left-hand periphery of his vision. It resembles a drawing of a firework, black lines to represent rays of light. Unlike a squib, the rays are not emitted but pulled in from the main view. It is called a scotoma, this black-and-white star that fizzes at the edge of everything Lear looks at. There is so much to look at.

A human figure's good for scale. Against the band of silver that is the Damodar river, the tall gipsy, the one from the banyan tree, will do. He appears again wearing ragged orange patchwork and plucking his zither. Lear takes the Claude glass and turns around, squinting. The gipsy throws his head back and bursts into song:

'*Khanchar bhitar Achin Pakhi kemne ase jay?*'

Lear jumps in shock, slipping down the bank. Over such a distance, 150 yards at least, it is as loud as a lion's roar. The loudest voice he's heard in years. The gipsy finishes his song and bows politely in their direction.

'What is he?' Lear asks Osman Ali.

'Sir, he is a minstrel, we call him a Baul. This one is known for his loudness. He is called Hathi. It means Elephant.' Quite informally, without mentioning payment, Osman Ali has become guide and interpreter for the morning. Lear can't help supposing Williams has sent him along to spy on them. Osman Ali doesn't interfere with Giorgio. Giorgio won't allow Osman Ali to help Lear back up the bank. That is his job. Lear, shaking, asks, 'What was that blast about?'

'It was about a bird.'

'It was enough to scare the birds. What kind of bird?'

'An unknown bird. That was its name, Achin Pakhi. Unknown Bird.'

'The Unknown Bird. And what about this Unknown Bird?'

'That once Hathi's chest became its birdcage and it sat beside his heart.'

'But could the poor thing breathe?'

Osman Ali (uncertain if the poor thing is the minstrel or the bird) continues: 'He left the door of the cage open and the Unknown Bird flew off. Now he is calling the bird back but he does not know its name. It is a sad song.'

'I should say so...'

Each verse ended by spinning itself out into a chain of little round vocables, sounding in chorus thus: 'Bo, bo-bo-bo, BO!'—and every verse was louder than its predecessor, till at the conclusion of the last verse, when the unearthly gypsy snatched off his crimson headcloth—glossy raven tresses at least three feet in length—& stamped his feet, the ground ringing with the frantic harmony—'Bo, bo-bo-bo, bo-bo-bo, bo-bo-bo, bobobo, BO!'—the last 'BO!' uttered like a pistol shot.

Two elephants are grazing on the river bank. Lear is greatly interested, peering at them through a little telescope. 'I like their backs, all hairy and covered in dust,' he tells Giorgio. He watches them lift clods of long grass from the ground, shaking the earth from the roots before popping them into their mouths. Sometimes they draw dust up into their trunks then spray it onto their backs. A deep grey-brown, a colour to be found in pebbles. Lear tells Giorgio and Osman Ali: 'People used to believe that elephants had no knees. They thought their legs were like columns. They couldn't bend or lie down. I don't suppose very many had ever seen an elephant, except in pictures. They thought that elephants slept leaning against trees. If you wanted to catch an elephant, you chopped down the tree it was sleeping against.'

That afternoon Lear makes drawings to amuse the two children. The children can barely decipher Lear's scrawled notes but the drawings are vivid enough. One is a picture of two birds sleeping in bed with a bolster. They have night-bonnets on. 'What is a chough?' asks Patience. In the second a gigantic owl, wearing spectacles just like Lear's own, sits atop a tiny tree smoking a churchwarden-pipe. In the third picture, a round-faced baby sleeps at the feet of a large nurse who takes up all the bed. Neither child is familiar with the rhyme but Patience says she has a doll that looks like the baby in the picture. It is made of wood and called Spoilt-Baby. It is a native doll, William says, coated in lacquer.

I thought I had worked out all the beauties of Taragunje, yet as much seems ahead as already done! (Did I note the blind beggar, who bumps his head and shakes his ribs and cries 'Babaa'?) As I walked along the river banks, I came all unawares on some temples and coco-palms, where a lot of Brahmins were eating, when one old fatty priest rose, priffing, and beckoned me off with signs of extreme disgust—so my shadow pollutes, I take it—Perhaps it does.

After dinner Lear sits with Williams in his private drawing-room. They are both a bit tipsy—Lear less so than his host, who has become voluble and expansive. How unwell Williams looks—his face is a ghastly khaki colour.

It is a stuffy little room, with a brass fender and rugs and a polished floor. There is a wooden coal bucket, decorated all around the sides with rustic pinecones. Lear's attention is drawn to a little black-framed water-colour, a large eye done all gelid and fishily with mock-Elizabethan script underneath, barely legible despite the size of the letters: 'Watch Over Us, O Lord.' Lear does not take the hotelier for a religious type, nor Mrs Williams.

'My father painted that, he painted occasionally,' explains Williams, waving his bandaged hand—whenever he thinks of his father, Williams sees an old white goat skittering about on a polished floor; he is waving the goat away—'Not portraits or landscapes. He painted upon spiritual conviction, his pictures were intended to enlighten people. My mother wouldn't let him hang them in the hotel. Most, I suppose, are somewhat didactic in nature. Sometimes he painted Glory...'

'And how was that?'

'The Glory pictures were largely white with yellow stripes to indicate celestial rays, very pale pictures like clouds...'

'Do you have one hanging anywhere that I may see?'

'That eye is the only picture of my father's I hang. The others are packed away. I do not find them pleasing to look at. My father was not trained as a painter, sir. He could not express, Mr Lear, what he meant. The paintings are inept. Guests would mock his daubs, I'm certain, and that would sadden me for he was sincere in making those pictures.'

Lear thinks this a pity; he is intrigued by the paintings of Glory. There are other paintings in the room. One is an oil of a black-and-tan dog of indeterminate breed, sitting on a parlour chair, making a withering expression; some pictures by trained but untalented painters, mainly of the sea and ships— East Indiamen on blue waters; a tea-clipper overtopping chalk cliffs, an improbably rocky island with a ruined church upon it and two tiny fishermen dragging an overscaled boat up a cliff.

Suddenly joyful, Williams claps his hands and says: 'Why don't you stay longer, Mr Lear? You could stay with us for Christmas?'

'You are very kind but I am invited to Calcutta.'

'To Government House?' Williams sounds incredulous.

Lear, a little irked to be doubted: 'I am invited as a friend of the Viceroy's. I have known him twenty-five years...'

'We are friends too, are we not?'

What a funny gent you are, William-Williams, thinks Lear and answers him smiling, 'Indeed we are, indeed we are.'

Ordinary politeness after all presumes friendliness, if not friendship. Williams accepts the affirmation quietly. Silence for a few minutes. Then Williams speaks, 'And if we were to walk abroad, in Taragunje or Calcutta, people would say there go two friends, would they not?'

'I cannot think why they shouldn't.' Soon, to his relief, they are discussing Lear's travels. Williams asks about Italy. Lear closes his eyes and sighs. He can picture it all: the mornings in the fresh meadows at the foot of the town, straying among the tall poplars wreathed with vines; the calm evenings, so full of incident; the return to the town at sunset with groups of peasants carrying up their corn, or parties of girls bearing each her own water-pot from the pure spring at the foot of the rock. The temperature feels the same, and the sound of insects and Williams could pass for the inn-keeper at Celano.

While Lear is reminiscing, the hotelier unwraps the bandage from his hand. Lear notices, with some alarm, that Williams has cut a deep gash across the swelling on his hand. The gash is caked in dried blood. Lear peers over his spectacles and asks, 'Should you have done that?'

'I could not stand to think of that poison inside me. Better to bleed it out.'

'Did it bleed dreadfully?'

'It bled for seventy-five minutes exactly, then it stopped. I rubbed the wound with alum crystal. I may assume all that creature's toxins left with the blood...'

'I should wrap it up again, if I were you. There's a good chap...'

Then Lear does not want to sit in the airless room any longer, with the wound on Williams' hand, and the lugubrious eye gleaming at him, and he stands up abruptly and announces his withdrawal.

> *Two large wings, one the punkah, the other its shadow, seemed like angels dimly moving, and some more prone to superstition than am I, might suppose a guardian spirit (e.g.–dear Ann's), watching.*

Osman Ali accompanies Lear and Giorgio to the station. The Calcutta train arrives like a bronze dragon, clanking and hissing in white mist. The open platform is crowded with people; clouds of steam from the engine and steam rising from kettles and boiling pots. The smell of hot oil and vegetable chops. Lear sees no other Europeans.

On the train, in the Second Class he prefers for short journeys, Lear is restless. He can't decide whether to face the engine or sit with his back to it, to eat the picnic the hotel has provided or buy bananas. He keeps shouting to Giorgio about plains and paddies and greens that darken not into brown but into grey. When Giorgio fails to understand, Lear raises his voice.

Giorgio is wary. It isn't good for his master to get so animated. The connecting phrases Lear mutters ('and then...', 'but...', 'so that...') are each accompanied by a movement. These movements are smooth and fluid–running his fingertips across his brow, wrapping his arms slowly about himself, crossing and uncrossing his knees–not alarming in any way. But when Lear's muscles rattle, in turn, one at a time, rattling first in a leg, then an arm, then a foot, and so on, then Lear is truly unwell. Giorgio is relieved when Lear starts scribbling in his notebook.

The half-English speech and queer ways of East-Indians. The gent was intelligent, the children also and we talked no end, though Mrs W opened her mouth not once. Flowers (send him some zinnia seeds from Calcutta). Roba sent to station. Then rather a hustle to get tickets for Calcutta, and luggage weighed. Off at 10.30. Flat plain. Dress of people here very feminine. Lunch: smashed eggs, cold fowl, bread and sherry. Farther on, two real live jackals. What greenery on all sides. What groups of figures. Crowded groves of bananas and all sorts of trees.

Lear twists in his seat. Giorgio watches him closely. Lear chews the end of his pencil, peering through the carriage window. 'Do not twist, please,' says Giorgio, '*stai creando troppo attenzione*'. Attention does not bother him but he knows Lear is prey to embarrassment. Giorgio, imperatively: 'Sit still.'

Two bespectacled Indian gentlemen, one in white lawn pajamas and the other in a green waistcoat, are sitting behind them. Both are advanced in years, the man in white haggard, the other taller, stouter and dark-skinned. They discourse in slow earnest English, which provokes Lear's curiosity.

'The eyes will be wide open,' intones the haggard man, 'with a constant upward gaze and the victim will feel shiveriness. There is stiffness of limbs, collection of phlegm in throat along with slurring of speech, almost to the state of delirium. Remember that the Crow is the *vahana* of Shani.'

Lear deduces they are physicians of some kind, working together on a lecture or an article. They are both referring to notes in their laps. The man in the green waistcoat takes up: 'In the *Kaphaja* type the onset of convulsions is delayed...'

'Wait. It is preceded, I think you will find, by...'

'It was coming next! And is preceded by an aura during which the patient feels cold and heavy and sees coloured objects as white. The seizure, when it arrives, is accompanied by falling and frothing at the mouth.'

'The fourth type, *Sannipatika*, is a combination of all of the above, is considered incurable, occurs in older people, and results in emaciation...'

'Emaciation....'

'Yes,' his voice rises in defence, 'E.. M.. A...'

'I think you mean death.'

'Emaciation, enfeeblement, then death. In that order.'

The speakers become aware that Lear is eavesdropping. They turn immediately to confront him. 'Excuse me, I beg you, please,' says Lear, 'I was interested that you speak English to one another'. Lear learns that the man in white speaks Bengali and Marathi, while the man in green speaks Tamil and Telugu. Both understand English, so that is their medium.

The Bengali lends Lear a Calcutta newspaper. Giorgio knows that a newspaper can provoke all kinds of wild behaviour in Lear who may weep at sad news, even throw himself about with happiness at good news.

Once in a *pensione* in Venice, reading in the *Times* that his friend Fortescue had been appointed Secretary of State for Ireland, Lear picked a fried whiting from the breakfast table to twirl about his head while he danced a hornpipe. The fish's body snapped from its tail and flew across the room, disturbing a party of American guests. Lear had apologised, explaining that he was celebrating good news, and the Americans with much bonhomie said they only regretted there were no fish on their table or they could twirl theirs too and dance their congratulations. Lear sees that Sir William Fairbairn has died—the news brings no special reaction.

4.35 Chandernagore; lovely! Lovely palms! Verdure always richer and richerer. O vegetatium! Lo! lovely river views!

Every minute makes life more wonderful. Astounding effects of beauty on each side railway, neck-twisting and eye-cracking!

At five-forty, the train reaches Howrah. Almost before the wheels have rolled to rest, the doors of their carriage are opened and a squadron of scarlet-coated Government House domestics burst in (alarming the medical gentlemen) to gather the bags and all the equipment while directing Lear and Giorgio to a steam launch on the bank of the Hooghly, just outside the vast whistling and hooting station. More Government House staff escort them as they chug across the river to a coach and four that will take them to Government House.

One of the horses pulling the coach stumbles on a hole in the road. It causes some delay and throws Lear into a panic. Giorgio reminds Lear to stay calm, in a pleasant temper, to meet his friends. '*Sei un uomo di dignita.*' All too often, in Giorgio's estimation, Lear is not even a human being: he changes shape, expands and contracts.

When people are happy and Lear is happy too, his shapelessness adds to the mirth; it rubs the edges from things, it is all of the same happy muddle, funny birds and feather-dusters, tickling people into wonder and laughter. When Lear is unhappy, he darkens into a small grey cloud with glinting spectacles; Giorgio could lead him away on a string, like a sad balloon.

4

With so many other British people at Government House, Lear is at his loneliest. He doesn't feel at one with his own kind, many of whom think the whole world English, or in a state of Anglicisation, the various nations aspiring to the glories of Shakespeare, hymns and cricket. These men go anywhere, performing imperial endeavours, certain of their lessons at Harrow and Haileybury. Lear's Englishness is itchier, less assured, and the world that he travels through most foreign to him; he prefers it foreign. It makes a better setting. The bearers at Government House have already noticed that his luggage is made in Rome and that he calls his luggage roba.

Instead of a room, Lear has been given a suite of rooms too magnificent to be comfortable. His bedroom is the size of an assembly hall, three vast windows on one side overlooking Calcutta, three more at the other side overlooking the great gate and entrance to Government House. On the table in his bedroom, among other volumes, is a copy of *Poor Miss Finch* by Lear's friend Wilkie Collins, published in London the previous year. Lear has not read this book, but he does know, from its serialisation in *Cassell's Magazine*, that one of the novel's protagonists has skin tinted blue by the silver nitrate he takes as medicine. Of course, it is easy to make too much of things like that—he is thinking of Williams with his yellow complexion.

An episode around teatime. Ann's voice again reading softly: 'Just now a beam of joy hung on his eyelash; but as I looked, it sunk into his eye like a bruised worm writhing its form of rings into a darkening hole...' Giorgio shoos the servants from Lear's rooms like so many chickens. He mutters, 'We must leave this Bengal. Is too humid for you. *Dovremmo trovare il deserto.*' Then he bolts the doors. The servants sit outside the doors with blank expressions but they hear every sound. They hear the men wrestling and they hear the Sahib splutter. Later, Giorgio emerges and tells them to let his master rest. He is wiping his brow. There is gossip, every kind of speculation.

Lord Northbrook, always kind and thoughtful, looks in and finds Lear propped up reading Trevelyan's *Cawnpore*. The Viceroy invites Lear to supervise the hanging of two of his own oil paintings after dinner. His Pyramid paintings are to hang in the Viceroy's private drawing room. 'Then stay and adjust them again, if need be, after a smoke with me.'

Lord Northbrook is a widower; his daughter Lady Emma is his companion and she is a dutiful girl, busy all the time, introducing people, organising excursions and games. It must be burdensome for such a young girl. Lear admires the way she gets on without a mother, she has retained all her goodness and simplicity. Emma, grown up, has less time for him and now Lear feels he is no more to her than an old family friend, a peculiar uncle. He finds it morbid that she wears her mother's dresses. In turn, she is not amused by him so readily any more. In Lucknow, he could not delight the girl once and she remarked, with a little impatience in her tone, that he trembled in the carriage.

After dinner, the Viceroy of India amuses himself by offering tidbits to his friend Lear's imagination:

'The principle of indivisibles is based on the assumption that any line may be divided up into an infinite number of points, each so tiny as to be immeasurable, a surface may be divided into an infinite number of lines, and a volume may be divided into an infinite number of surfaces. All matter, in other words, is composed of an infinite number of immeasurably thin planes. And that includes us, of course...'

Lear splutters with amusement: 'So I am a pile of very thin wafers! Am I wise to walk along Chowringhee? Won't I get toppled?'

'But Chowringhee itself is made of planes.'

'Nothing is solid!'

Evelyn Baring joins them. Lear calls him 'Young Baring' to distinguish him from the Viceroy whose surname is the same. He is the Viceroy's cousin and Private Secretary and not particularly young any more, moving in his career from promise to distinction. He too has known Lear for many years—earlier in a posting in Corfu, he had found Lear delightful at his best, but more often tragic and ridiculous. Nine years later, he finds an older stouter Lear a little daunting. Lear breathes audibly through his nostrils when Baring stands beside him. Baring runs over his cousin's advice. 'He is best taken, I feel, as an articulate and gifted child, full of wonder, astonishment, comedy—but not quite a grown-up...' What of the Albanian? 'His nurse, don't you see?' He does not stray far from his nurse. It is almost comical, yet Baring feels a tenderness for the innocent old gent, the desire to protect him on his way. Once in Corfu Lear had sent him a letter, written in a sort of code that Baring never cracked: *thrippsy pillivinx, inky tinky pobblebookle abblesqabs? Flosky!* And so on. It had made no sense and it hadn't been all that funny. Baring wonders if Lear remembers that letter; he writes so many.

Lord Northbrook is telling Lear: 'What Descartes says is that the mind and the brain are two separate things. The brain is physical matter, a muscle more or less—whereas the mind is shapeless, insubstantial...'

'So where is it?' asks Lear.

'Oh, it emanates from the brain,' the Viceroy reassures him. 'The pineal gland, no bigger than a pea, inside the brain...' Lear sees this gland as a hinge that links body and soul. Far from shapeless, the mind Lear pictures is like a huge half-inflated air-balloon, or a flyaway tent, or a suitcase flung open. A billowing thing that trails him like a ghost.

'The pineal gland is only found in human beings,' states the Viceroy.

'Well, I know a cat has a mind,' says Lear, 'whether it has a pineal gland or not. I know they think. I've often watched my cat think.'

'Cats have brains, of course...'

'Don't they think with their brains?' asks Lear.

Lord Northbrook nods: 'Up to a degree.'

'I don't understand at all. If the brain thinks, what does the mind do?'

'It thinks about thinking—puts it all in place—so to speak.'

It is getting a little precipitous for Lear; he is just clinging on: 'Is the mind the same thing as the soul?'

'That I haven't fathomed myself,' says the Viceroy solemnly, as if feeling his bereavement. 'I can't comment, really.'

Lear tells them about his brother Charles who went to the Fever Coast as a medical missionary. He caught the fever within months of arrival. The kind natives saw him to a British ship but the Captain said Charles was too ill to travel unattended. An African woman called Adjouah volunteered to tend him. Charles was so overcome by her kindness that he married Adjouah, there and then, despite his feverish condition. When he got back to London, he regretted his haste and dispatched Adjouah (who, though regarded as a woman in her own country, was fourteen years old) to his married sister Eleanor Newsom, who was without children, in Leatherhead. Adjouah was sent to school for three years. Charles, all the while, had raised funds to return to the Fever Coast. After five years, he died there. Lear has no idea where in Western Africa he died.

'How sad,' says Baring. 'I expect you miss him.'

'I miss his hands at the piano, that's all. He had spatulate fingers with big blunt tips. You never saw such fingers.'

Charles could have gone anywhere, he never told anyone where he was going. When Adjouah learned that her husband had died, she saw no reason to remain in Leatherhead. She sailed back to the Fever Coast.

'Does she write to your sister?' asks the Viceroy.

'No, it's a pity. I expect she's a missionary herself now.'

'Perhaps she has shed her faith.'

'Who knows?'

'Perhaps she found Christianity irrelevant beyond Leatherhead,' says the Viceroy.

Lear smokes until twelve, declares the positioning of the pictures satisfactory, then retires to find Giorgio waiting up for him. '*V'a letto*,' Lear tells him in a muffled voice.

> Mrs Jaypher said it's safer
> If you've lemons in your head
> First to eat a pound of meat
> And then to go at once to bed.

There are no lemons in Lear's head but hundreds of bright copper wheels, all spinning rapidly. The wheels are without cogs.

He still senses, as he has throughout his life, that he lacks the experience and knowledge necessary to achieve the beginning of an understanding. As he has gained knowledge from life, he feels that it is like a puddle that spreads without gaining depth. He feels that other minds go deeper: pools instead of puddles, even lakes.

5

---

*C*alcutta draws investors, speculators and moneylenders from all over. Gold and silver coins swim like shiny fish through Calcutta, up the river and down the river, over the seas. Real wealth is solid. The way to hold on to money is to turn the piles of gold mohurs into bricks. The Deys cleared the bazaar that had grown around their palace walls and erected pukka houses, shops and godowns. They bought land from zamindars across north Calcutta, landlords too stricken by misfortune to run their estates efficiently. The Deys built more houses, shops and godowns. The rents came in. The bazaar came back to Burrapoker, squeezing its ragged awnings into the spaces left open. It is allowed to stay because it provides a bed of gossip and a source of information. The family retains so much information: the various circumstances of the tenants, the circumstances reported of others, all the relative triumphs and disappointments of their lives. The family have backed British ventures across the subcontinent, the Dey fortunes going into tea, cotton, jute, indigo and coal. With the return from their investments, they have bought bighas of land around the villages of their ancestors and built their country house, Bhavani Place.

In 1823 (the year of Dey's birth) a list called *The Respected and Opulent Natives of the Presidency* was published in Calcutta. It named twenty-three families, as well as eighty-four unmarried gentlemen, residing in various quarters of the city. The Deys of Barapukur were included. They are considered *banedi*, that is 'of the foundation'. Matilal Chandranath Dey, the first Raja, had been given the land in north Calcutta upon which the family's palaces stand by the East India Company. He had been living in Gobindapur before it was cleared to build the new Fort William. The land near Sutanuti was his compensation. The Company also awarded Matilal his royal patent, their prerogative when granting land. Matilal paid for the *bara pukur*, the 'large tank' that gives the district its name. The tank is still there a century later, not especially large but perhaps larger than other tanks in that part of Calcutta. Matilal's fortune came from textiles (muslins and calicos) that he supplied to the British and later to the American merchants. The Deys descend from scriveners, Kayasths, men of words. The Kayasths knew Sanskrit as well as the Brahmins but were record-keepers rather than priests. When the Mughals reached Bengal, the Kayasths learned Persian and Arabic. As translators and then commercial intermediaries, they prospered. When the British arrived, the Kayasths learned English. It was in their nature. Matilal came south from the red uplands, to act as a comprador. It is Dey's opinion that his grandfather lived in an age of enchantment, when to speak English was all that was needed. He claims all the banedi fortunes are based on luck. He also claims savvy is inherited and that again is luck. 'Quite a lot of the differences between rich and poor are matters just of luck. To revel in one's privilege would be foolish. Even more foolish would be to suppose the rich work harder than the others.' Dey works very little but exercises instead a commanding sloth. He is not dismissive of luck. It is a boon from the gods. Dey gives his support to the Society for the Promotion of National Feeling. He speaks of *Sonar Bangla*. It means Golden Bengal. He started by imagining Golden Bengal as all the centuries before the Muslims and before the British. In that Sonar Bangla, his unsentimental mind tells him,

Kayasths never prospered. There was no need for other languages. Kayasths could only be scribes. So now he imagines Sonar Bangla as the Golden Future of Bengal.

Recently, Dey has started to collect photographs. He is not interested in photography as a means of artistic expression but as documentation. He is intrigued by the lack of emotion in photographs: it is the eye of a camera, a mechanical truth. They are not pictures but facts to him, statements from the immediate past. Folders are sent regularly from Petrocochino, Bourne & Shepherd and other studios in the city. His collection started with views of Calcutta. The streets always seem unpeopled. Dey remarks upon this to the salesman who explains that the camera can't record motion. Dey often wonders if things exist when he's not looking at them. Photography (*chhayachitra*, he calls it) sets his thoughts spinning along melancholy philosophical strings towards a tangled, almost inexpressible, state of acceptance, a knot that cannot be untied. He collects photographs of trees. He isn't sure what draws him to trees, unless it is his father Balendra's love of them, but he enjoys the leaves in the photographs, that seem like flames when they dance out of focus. He has no desire to take photographs himself. A cousin, Nilmadhab Dey, has made a name for himself in photographic portraits. Nilmadhab's portrait photographs are to Dey less satisfactory than painted portraits. He notices that the light ages the sitter, the temporary creases in a face are rendered permanent, and people look emptier, with nothing inside the skin. Chhayachitra, shadow pictures. That morning, he has sent seventy-five photographs to be mounted, glazed and framed.

His customary manner is to conceal his emotions, but when Dey learns Lear is in India and that he is staying at Government House, he shuffles over the carpets like a mandarin in his excitement. The information, passed to Dey through a spider's web of gossip and mutterings, is confirmed by Government House servants. He wants to know everything about the mysterious painter, creator of his favourite painting and author of the puzzling poems.

'He does not travel alone, Master. We hear he has a white servant.'

'Is that so odd?' asks Dey.

'It is unusual,' says the informant, who is dressed in white cotton.

'I shall take my servants when I am summoned to London,' says Dey. 'English servants wouldn't know how to dress me.' He would need to dress splendidly at the Court of Saint James.

'That would be necessary, Master,' agrees the informant, 'but it is not necessary for an Englishman to bring a servant here'.

'I suppose not.'

'Unless there is more to it.'

'What do the servants at Government House say?' Dey settles, like an actor, upon a day-bed.

'It is a question of interpretation, Master.'

For a long time, Dey rests his arm on the cushion of the divan and studies his reflection in the Belgian mirror. The informant hovers, waiting for his benefactor to speak. Dey is not especially vain; he finds staring at his reflection helpful to concentrate his thoughts.

'You have ascertained that there was such a king?'

'Doctor Beardshaw of Presidency College,' says the informant with some reverence, 'cited Geoffrey of Monmouth. Long before Shakespeare, he assures me. He told me Lear was the son of Bladud, who was descended from Brutus.'

'Who were these people?'

'Very ancient English kings.'

The Dey family inhabit two palaces in Burrapoker Street, their Calcutta home. The Old Palace was built in the last quarter of the eighteenth century. From the street it looks plain enough but once you pass through its gates, which are large enough for elephants to pass through, its grandeur is evident: five mahals strung in a row and the *thakur dalan* ('hall of the gods') in the style called Bengal Adam. The family emblem of a full moon rising above an unfurled scroll is repeated in plaster or marble relief throughout both palaces. The New Palace, where most of the Deys live, is less Indian altogether. A clock decorates the gateway; beneath it in marble is the scroll of the family crest, in this instance the moon has become the Cooke & Kelvey clockface. The paired columns are Tuscan on the ground floor and Ionic at the first-floor level, correctly Vitruvian according to Balendra Chandranath Dey, its architect.

A foreign visitor might suppose the thakur dalan at the Old Palace to be a theatre: at one end there is a dais like a little covered stage. The thakur dalan has classical nymphs beside the stage; on the right side there is a statue of Napoleon, on the left, one of Shakespeare. All through the winter Pujas, effigies of various gods and goddesses are placed upon the dais, attended by priests who perform long elaborate rites at auspicious hours. Friends and relatives of the Dey family attend the rites and celebrate. There might be musicians. Dey does not necessarily attend all these occasions. He often shuts himself in the library. Instead of reading he stares at the wall, chewing rhythmically on slivers of betel.

⁎ ⁍

Dey has a vivid and distressing memory of an event that happened in the jungle around Bhavani Place, when he was a child. The memory is frayed at the edges, so it starts and ends with flashes.

An elephant trunk carved from black stone, a waterspout shaped like a goat's head, a wrought-iron garden bench with one collapsed arm, a terrace of knitted stones. The light, panicky movement of squirrels, the call of the wood pigeon, dapples of sunshine in the gaps between branches, knots of chameli blossom in a waterless fountain, the dahuk bird above, the crackling sound of a chameleon moving in the dried leaves. Ancient mahogany trees, fig trees, neem, gulmohar, growing wild everywhere. A thick undergrowth of fern and thorny shrubs, interlaced with wild brambly roses, spread like a carpet.

He was walking with his father, Balendra. Deep in the woods they had discovered a few houses batched together, a small village. A gang of children came rushing towards them. The children had paint on their faces and chests and carried bows. Dey started to cry. His father reassured him: the children were *bahurupis*; they were actors. One of the bahurupis recited a verse about Ram and Laxman while the others pranced about, enacting the story, imitating gods and animals. Dey was fretting that they would be asked to pay for the performance: they had no money with them. An adult joined the bahurupis, a dwarf, no taller than the children and without paint. Everyone ignored the dwarf except Dey. The dwarf, in turn, stared straight at Balendra. He danced, lunging towards the visitors. He swung his arms and leapt at Balendra's chest. Dey tried to help his father, who fell backwards onto him. He can still see the circling trees and the branches opening like hands and his father's back rattling. He remembers the red earth breaking into hundreds of tiny cubes and the shrill cry of a bird. He shouts out, 'That bird!'

'What bird is it?' asks Shyamali, disturbed by his anxious state.

'It is always the same bird. I don't hear it otherwise.'

'Is it a tok-tok bird?'

'I don't know what bird it is,' he snaps.

In an illustrated edition of Abbé Dubois' *Hindu Manners, Customs and Ceremonies* Dey looks at the *Ananda Tandava*, Lord Shiva's Dance of Bliss. Lord Shiva's eyes are sleepy but watchful, like a cat's. In his hair is a snake, a sickle moon, a mermaid to represent the river Ganges, and a skull. He wears earrings: the right one a penis, the left a vagina. He stays quite calm while performing the most frantic dance on a lotus flower. It is, Dey understands, a dance of triumph. Lord Shiva leaps and twirls in a hoop of flame, to the beat of a small drum in his upper right hand. Lord Shiva opens the palm of his upper left hand to let a small flame jump from it. With his lower right hand he makes the gesture of *abhaya*, divine protection, while his lower left arm stretches diagonally across and out from his body like an elephant's trunk. It is the gesture a dancer makes to indicate strength. A finger of that hand points down to his raised left foot and the broken body of the demon Apasmara.

Long ago in a pine forest there lived a community of sages. Vanity had undermined their convictions, and their rituals had become pompous and empty. What's more, they demanded the most beautiful girls in the locality be given to them as wives. Lord Shiva, to teach them a lesson, went to the pine forest. He arrived on the riverbank just as the wives were bathing. He danced on the ghat and the woman shrieked when they saw him. 'Please don't cover yourselves on my behalf,' he told them. The girls laughed and displayed themselves to the god's seductive eyes. When the sages returned from their rituals, the wives innocently recounted Lord Shiva's dance at the riverbank. That night the sages gathered around a ceremonial fire, their powers restored by anger. They conjured a great tiger from the flames. It sprang at Lord Shiva, who skinned it with the nail of his little finger. He wound the skin about his waist as a loincloth. The sages conjured a flying trident from the fire. Lord Shiva caught it in his right hand. They conjured countless serpents from the fire. Snake after snake, Lord Shiva wove into his hair or draped about his shoulders as ornaments. Finally they summoned, from the cinders at the edge of the fire, the demon Apasmara, a dark deformed dwarf, the enemy of words and memories.

Apasmara threw a fireball at Lord Shiva, who drew the glowing rocket into a small flame that danced on the palm of his hand. Then he stamped on Apasmara's back, breaking it like damp, rotten wood. Lord Shiva's acts are constantly taking place: he may have broken Apasmara's back but he is still to break Apasmara's back. It has happened and it is always about to happen.

In the meantime, Apasmara rampages. Apasmara has victims all over Bengal. He jumps on their backs and grabs their necks and tries to pull their heads off. Usually, the victim shakes him off but Apasmara is persistent and cunning. The demon wants to pull the heads from people's shoulders or reach inside their mouths to grab their tongues. He goes for tongues. Apasmara chose Balendra because he had designed the libraries. Words swarmed around Dey's father like gnats. When Balendra looked at a flower, he saw the flower and its name. He would turn a thought into a sentence before considering it. When he spoke English, he saw the Bengali word jump and change shape for its new setting. A phrenologist declared that Balendra had a sac filled with words hanging from his brain. Some years later, Dey asked his mother about the sac. 'How did he know it was filled with words?'

'You could put your ear to the back of his head and hear them,' said his mother.

'What did they sound like?'

'Hundreds of voices whispering at once.'

The attacks increased. There were so many places for a demon to hide in Calcutta. He could jump on Balendra from roofs and high windows. He could lurk in a bookshop or a theatre. He could hide in the bamboo scaffolding of the New Palace. Balendra felt he would be safer in the country. He moved with his wife and son to Bhavani Place, but in the cold months the family always returned to Burrapoker Street.

In the hot weather before the monsoon, they found Balendra lying in the shade of a gaub tree, his kurta stained with blood and his dhoti soiled. The smell had brought flies. Balendra's tongue hung ragged from his mouth. His face wasn't pale in death but indigo blue, with a pink rag hanging from it. This is how Dey sees his dead father, from his mother's description. Dey knows the gaub tree, the dry leaves beneath it, because he walked through those woods with Balendra. His father told him the names of trees: palas, sondal, gulmohar. Dey would look up into the branches for him. Apasmara is supposed to be invisible to all but his victims. They sense when he is around because the air starts fizzing. Apasmara is described as a fireball or the glare of the sun. As a child, Dey could see his father's demon plainly. His mother told him never to mention that to anybody in the palace, never to the servants. 'Listen to me. Nobody can see Apasmara except his victims. Your father told you about him, that was all. You, Pannalal, could not have seen him.' He remembers her voice, strained with urgency.

When Apasmara killed his father, Dey was not there. Dey has never seen Apasmara again. He watches out for dwarves, avoiding them when possible. The palace servants know of the Raja's dislike of dwarves; they see it as an eccentricity, possibly a superstition. His wife Shyamali knows only that Dey's childhood was disturbed by his father's death. It accounts for his melancholy, his way of turning life into gloomy ritual.

He withdraws into himself, like a book shutting with a soft thud. Intellectual endeavour, Shyamali believes, banishes despondency. For all his reading, she feels her husband is afraid of books, he just sits among them as if in a nest.

6

A plate of sliced melon is brought to Lear's rooms. Lear eats some at once. Giorgio refuses to take any. Lear insists that the fruit is pure and wholesome.

'*Come conoscete questo*?' asks Giorgio.

He believes the air in Calcutta is bad for his master's health. In his opinion, Lear is less at risk the thinner and drier the air. Lear ignores Giorgio's suggestions, dismisses his theories as folklore. When Lear insists again that he eat some melon, Giorgio stares him right in the eye: 'No, *vorrei mangiare cipolle...*'

'Very well then,' says Lear, white with anger. He rings the little bell.

A servant arrives and Lear asks for a plate of onions, peeled but not sliced.

Silence. After five minutes, the servant returns, with the onions.

Lear points to the plate. Giorgio takes an onion and places it on the marble chimneypiece. He clenches his right hand into a fist and smashes it down on the onion, which bursts apart in irregular fragments. Lear clutches his heart in an exaggerated theatrical way, then smiles. It is a private merriment. Smiling too, Giorgio bites into a piece. 'I beat the onion to sweeten it...'

Lear and Giorgio are startled by the adjutant cranes they see perching on roofs or ambling along the pavements. Monstrous cranes the size of grown men, with beaks a yard long, bald heads and huge crops of red wrinkly flesh. They encounter a pair of adjutants in Middleton Row. Should they lift their hats? Giorgio insists they are a species of vulture, calls them *sporchi avvoltoi*. On Christmas Eve Lear notices a row of adjutant cranes lining up beside the Cathedral. Anything lined up appeals to his humour. He usually takes a sketchbook on his walks. For drawing Lear prefers the Botanical Gardens, with the banyan even bigger than that at Taragunje, a colossus the size of a village. Best of all, the native quarters of Calcutta, especially the southern edges of the city that fray into jungle and vegetable gardens.

Scrawl: We get tea very early, also toast and butter, the latter in a dab on the side of the plate, never eaten. Drove to Tollygunje; a lovely morning, yet very chilly. Beautiful bits of village and verdure; I do not think I ever before saw so much novel, interesting and drawable stuff in so small a space and so short a time. First trial of Martin-Bowley's new boots. Strange to say my heel was not bothered but tight across the toes. How gorgeous is the colouring of this east, qua draperies, etc. Still the kettle-mending bird works away! What long-legged goats are here, out on the yellow environs. Remark the beauty of white sheets, both in light and shadow–also black bodies and white waist cloths–also, extreme featheriness, of Cocoa nut Palms;–depths of brown grey shade;–brilliancy of Bananas, and general misty greyness, more like English even than Nile scenes at early morning–owing to the profusion of vegetation, whereas Egyptian ditto is scanty and less deep. The shadows in the Tank might be done from Elms or Oaks. General tone of the Mosque and Tank view, deep beautiful dark grey, relieved with vividly bright bits of light;–a green tone throughout;–even the Mosque domes are rather greeny brown. The palms, if in shadow–have hardly any colour. Walk on slowly,–drawing at times. Endlessly beautiful

pictures of village life and Eastern vegetation. Tok-Tok or
tempest bird heard for the first time today; he is a barbet.
Back by nine; prayers, breakfast.

A letter is delivered to Lear on a silver tray by a splendid
servant wearing a sash. A Christmas message, he supposes. It is
an invitation from Raja Pannalal Chandranath Dey to the
Burrapoker Palace in Burrapoker Street, there to discuss a
commission to paint the lands around the Raja's country
residence, Bhavani Place. The letter shows some knowledge of
Lear's career, for this Raja claims to own a painting of Lear's
called *Philae at Sunset*, a painting he made some twenty years
earlier. He made many versions of that picture. The first one
had been sold to the Duc d'Aumale who lived at Twickenham.
At certain times Lear has made as many as twenty copies of a
painting. He calls these copies Tyrants, because they tire him
so. Lear takes the letter as merriment for Christmas, a sample
of the particular humour to be found among the British in
Calcutta, when they try to be Nonsensical. It is a little
embarrassing, not something he enjoys. Only Giorgio and Lord
Northbrook make him laugh at present.

7

A dark grey line, a phenomenon of the cool weather, hangs in the air above the roofs and the goods-yards and the tall heaps of coal. There hasn't been a guest at Williams Hotel since Lear departed. Osman Ali has disappeared. Another bearer, Williams assures his wife, will come forward; you may rely on the bush telegraph; the word goes from household to household. Europeans are always moving out of station, going home, dying. 'It won't take long,' he assures his wife.

Fever raises the heat of the blood, the heat of the bowels. Poor Williams suffers horribly. There is the constant flux and now he's concerned about his memory. It seems to be affected by the heat of his blood as well, so there are days he passes that do not enter his record properly and he could only tell you he was ill, little or nothing else. If the ear shall say, because I am not the eye, I am not of the body; is it therefore not of the body? If the whole body were an eye, where was the hearing? And if the whole were hearing, where were the smelling? He decides to send Lear the tube of drawings Moore left behind.

Whenever he is strong enough, Williams attends his flowers. The monkeys have not been back. There are new buds. Old Banamali follows all his instructions about watering and feeding. Williams consults his father's garden notebook.

> *Grubs.—These are for the most part the larvæ of beetles. The ravage they commit is almost entirely confined to the roots of potted plants, in eating away the fibrous parts, and thus ultimately causing the plants to perish. They are generally introduced in the cow-manure when the plants are potted. Occasional top-dressings of gas lime are useful. The application of creosoted soil is beneficial.*

> *Parrots.—The little green parrot is a most destructive bird to ripening fruit, unless nets be thrown over the trees to keep it off.*

He is impressed by his father's clerical hand. The instructions are concise, soldierly, campaigning against all adversity. He holds this image of his father in his mind for a moment. Then the picture starts to crumble. A tuft of coarse white hair breaks through, the tip of a pointed tongue, a pair of asymmetrical horns...

Mrs Williams has a folding table positioned in the hall of the hotel. Upon this table she places a shallow tin tray that is covered by an even layer of soil. Over the soil, she scatters millet seed and every day William and Patience water the seeds with a small silver can. On the twenty-second, a wooden stable is set up on the greensward of millet, and plaster figures of the Nativity are set in place by the children. A star of golden paper is set atop the stable. Just last year, it was admired by all the guests. This Christmas, there are none. The crib is admired only by the servants. The decorations go up, the Chinese streamers and the bunting. A great bough cut by Banamali from the Child's Life tree is brought to the hall and planted in a zinc-tub of soil. The children decorate its many branches with baubles and tinsel, and candles in thin brass holders are fastened here and there, and another gold star, even larger, at the tip. Williams, who is not a religious man any longer, holds to the details of the rituals but only as straws to clutch at.

Flying Foxes.—These commit their depredations by night. A net is the only safeguard against them.

Squirrels; Baboons.—These animals are sometimes very destructive and must be scared off.

'Cyanogas'—(Calcium Cyanide) a proprietary product of the American Cyanamide Co., can be got in tins as dust or granules. Sulphur can be obtained as ground sulphur, flowers of sulphur or milk of sulphur.

One afternoon while the crib is on display, Williams finds himself out among the paddies at the edge of the town. He is wearing his father's wide-awake hat. He has no recollection of walking in that direction, nor of setting off from the hotel. He is dressed in his long nightshirt, over which he has buttoned a black swallow-tail coat. On his feet are patent leather slippers. He has no recollection of dressing and he would never go about in such outlandish garb. Some men are working in the paddies. As Williams passes, he asks in Bengali, 'What rice is this?'

'*Boro dhan.* Winter rice, of course.'

'How does it harvest?' Williams knows nothing of farming but something of figures. Peasants are generally numerate, in his experience. Figures might provide a dialogue. Why the situation merits an exchange of figures, he doesn't know. It is a way of getting at facts, clutching at straws again.

'Fifty or sixty maunds...'

'A kottah?'

'A kottah! If a kottah could yield fifty maunds of grain, the living would be easy. A bigha, of course.'

Great laughter all round. It dawns on Williams that they have taken him for an Indian in his strange attire. He says, 'I have lived nearby for many years but I was born in Wales.'

One man asks, 'Where is this village? What do you call it? Wollish?'

'Wales. It is not a village, it is a country.' He resorts to loud English: 'My name is Williams. I am the owner and proprietor of Williams Hotel.'

The men understand enough English to stop mocking him. One, in his own language, says, 'Sahib. You speak such flawless Bangla, we took you for a babu from the city. Please, forgive our misunderstanding. We do not come from here.'

Williams replies in Bengali: 'How could I possibly resemble an Indian?'

The men laugh again but more politely this time. 'We are working in the glare of the sun, Sahib, it ruins our eyes.'

As Williams walks back to his hotel, a nursery song wriggles through his memory like a worm. Over and over he can hear its irritating tune—if he doesn't clench his jaws, he would sing it aloud:

The cuckoo's a bonny bird, he sings when he flies,
He brings us good tidings, and he tells us no lies;
He sucks little birds' eggs to make his voice clear,
And he never cries coo-coo till the summer draws near.

Williams does not tell his wife of the episode: he can already see her reaction. At such times he misses Osman Ali. There is nobody to talk to any more.

On Christmas Eve, a parcel arrives at the hotel from Calcutta. It comes from Lear and contains various packets of flower seeds from Hogg Market and a book of *Nonsense Songs, Stories, Botany and Alphabets*. There is a kind note as well. Williams looks upon Lear's visit as an interlude of clarity in a confused time.

At sunset—a guest at Williams Hotel!

It is Slingsby Moore.

Williams slaps the back of a chair, sending dust flying. He holds himself tall: 'I trust you have come to pay your bill, Mr Moore.'

Slingsby Moore shuffles beside his bag in the hall. He has lost weight since Williams last saw him. He is hatless and bald, the top of his head is pink and covered in peeling blisters. He speaks in a dry *pizzicato*, as if reserving the full range of his voice for better company: 'I have all that and more.' Williams notices Moore's bulging eyes and shuffling movements, his constant expression of angry surprise. Moore takes a large pile of banknotes from the pocket of his coat. 'This looks a great deal but it has to last me until I find work in Calcutta.'

Williams kicks the skirting board. A small shower of plaster comes down from the ceiling. 'If you stay, you must pay in advance.'

'I should be happy to.'

'Have you no more baggage?'

'Everything has been taken from me...'

Williams kicks the skirting board again—no plaster this time. 'Were you robbed?'

'Yes, in a sense...'

Williams says, 'You left some pictures here. I sent them on to Calcutta, to a painter called Lear, of your acquaintance he told me. I thought he was more likely to meet you than I was. You will admit, your reappearance is unexpected.'

'Lear? Lear? Who's he? King Lear.' Moore dimly recalls a brimming winecup and a reeking pipe; a conversation with a Cockney owl.

'Do not be facetious, Sir. He is an honest gentleman.'

Moore is led to his room by young Selim, a boy from the kitchen. Moore has left a book on the reception table. Williams picks it up. It is bound in blue leather; 'Beddoes' in punched letters. He opens it and reads one line (about snakes of silver throat) before Moore rushes back and snatches the book away. 'I'll have that, thank you. I know well what happens to books around here.' Williams, who has seen many a book devoured by white ants, wants to ask: Have you seen a dictionary transformed into lace? Have you seen the works of

Maria Edgeworth made into powder? But he thinks the less he says the better. To distract himself, he looks in his father's book.

White Ants;—A greater inconvenience in this Country is the infinite number of white ants, which though they are but little, have teeth so sharp, they will eat down a wooden stool in a short time. And if great care is not taken in the places where you lock up your linen, in two days they will eat through a pile of bedsheets, as if it had been sawn in two down the middle. Whenever found, their nests must be destroyed and the Queen-White-Ant killed. This must be done before the others, so it is an Execution.

8

---

*T*he grander parts of Calcutta are too English—
Chowringhee is a disappointment. Lear had expected an
oriental Promenade des Anglais. He finds instead an oriental
Cheltenham, where dismal yellow dogs stalk the gutters.
Giorgio, on the other hand, finds echoes of Corfu Town in
Calcutta: the classical British buildings; the Maidan flanked by
Fort William and Government House remind him of the
Esplanade in Corfu overlooked by the Old Fort. Just as
Chowringhee runs by the side of the Maidan, so the Liston,
with its cafés and fashionable emporia, edges the Esplanade.
In both parks: cricket and statues of dignitaries. Lear and
Giorgio walk by the river 'mooning', as Lear calls the
disengaged but intensely observant way he walks the crowded
paths. They pass bathing ghats and shrines attended by
ferocious-looking mendicants or *gosains* with matted manes
and fiery eyes. Some, to devilish effect, carry tridents. Giorgio
scrutinises the fishing-nets. They pass through a flower market.

By Prinsep Ghat, a young woman steps from a tiny blue
temple and beckons with a cupped hand. She is cradling a
rigid baby in her arms. On closer inspection, Lear sees that it
is actually a wooden doll. The woman unwraps the doll for
them. It is a hideous black wooden thing with the body and six
limbs of a cockroach and the face of a depraved toddler. Lear
hears these words: 'If there were dreams to sell, what would

you buy? Some cost a passing bell, some a light sigh...' It is his sister's voice, reading to him. He hands a few coins to the woman. Inside the temple, they observe a Hindoo ritual: two chanting priests cracking coconuts on a hatter's block. When they emerge, a small crowd has assembled to watch a show put on by men from the fishermen's colony, they are told by a willowy youth who offers to translate the Bengali words for them.

A performer wearing a white mask and a red horsehair wig, an officer's coat and an opera hat, represents an Englishman. He bellows for his servant who arrives running, bowed and subservient.

'Backwards, *ek do*!' roars the Englishman and the servant retraces his actions, bowing and rising away from his master who shouts, 'Forwards, *ek do*!'

The servant goes back and forth like a toy monkey on a wheel until the Englishman tires of the fun and calls for brandy, which the servant brings in a large green bottle and pours straight into his mouth. The translator adds, 'This is not to offend your good self...' Intoxicated, the Englishman swaggers about, attempting to dance a hornpipe. The musicians start playing their pipes and drums. The servant is ordered to dance but muddles the steps. The Englishman beats him with the brandy bottle until he collapses. His wife arrives, a tall flaxen-headed ashen-faced woman played by a man. The Englishman, keeping his hat on, throws her into a rough waltz, drags her through a quadrille until she collapses. At this, he breaks into song: 'I punish my servant and I punish my wife. *Ta dhin ta dhin nachi ami.* Beat the drum! Let me dance! I'm the King of Trifle Gardens.'

In Bentinck Street Lear equips them both with body belts. There isn't time for Lear to have a coat made. The ready-made garments on offer have plainly been dashed up on the cheap for fellows in a hurry to the tea gardens. The cloth is thin and the seams bulge. Instead, Lear buys a buff blanket with heather-coloured stripes, to wrap about himself in the lower Himalayas.

'Sahib, this is for the bed,' the blanket-seller advises him, 'not for wearing purposes'. But Lear thinks it just the thing for the hills.

And all the way along the Esplanade men keep rushing up, offering their services as trained waiters and sous-chefs. Many have trained at establishments with Italian names like Firpo's and Peliti's. 'I am not a restaurateur,' Lear tells them forlornly. 'Just a dirty landscape painter.' An old man says that he is a specialised painter's bearer, the son of the Daniells' specialised bearer. Lear admires the Daniells' pictures but finds their views strangely unpeopled: where are the men in their swarms? Lear says he has an assistant; his companion is his assistant. The men keep their distance after that. Some stand back, making clucking sounds. Lear ignores them but asks himself why some travellers are respected wherever they go whilst others face nothing but ridicule. A coincidence: Osman Ali from Taragunje, plainly recognisable in the mocking crowd. Why does he not come forward?

He tells Young Baring about the Burrapoker letter. It turns out that the invitation is real: there is such a Raja. Baring can vouch for the Dey family. Good eggs, helpful to British interests, public-spirited. Baring informs Lear that the Raja is essentially a merchant prince, quite unlike the bejewelled royalty Lear encountered in Lucknow. 'Altogether cannier, less comic opera.'

He thinks the note of flippancy appropriate for his cousin's artistic friend. 'Oh,' Lear replies with a perfectly round mouth framed in his beard. It is meant to indicate understanding but it flusters Baring. He wonders if Lear knows something he doesn't. He remembers the Viceroy commenting that Lear was the most unknowable of all his friends.

Lear decides there and then he will go to Burrapoker Street to make the arrangements. A watercolour painting could be executed in situ; a work in oil would have to be sent later from Europe. He reminds himself not to harp on the price: he's been advised it makes a customer apprehensive. 'But I am the apprehensive one,' Lear would protest.

All over the lawns of Government House Lear can see crows gathering in their hordes. When Lear is uneasy, India seems infested with the noisy creatures. Their racket is everywhere, all day long. Recently, in Lucknow, Lear visited a bird market where crows were sold from cages. Who, he asked his guide, would buy a crow, when they are everywhere? The guide replied, both Hindus and Muslims. There is an ancient and popular science called *Vayasa-Vidya*. It is the knowledge of crow language, understanding the caws and, to a lesser extent, the patterns they make in flight. To learn the language, it is necessary to live close to a crow. It takes long stretches of concentration and the suspension of all other thoughts. The guide explained that the crow knows three great secrets; immortality, the origin of things—for the crow was the only bird to witness creation—and the nature of Hell, having lived there some time in another age. The crow's nature is deceitful, so only the wisest pandits may decide when a crow's statement is to be believed or disregarded. It may even be that the crow consulted in the first place was deceitful.

Lear, who is dressing for dinner, looks at the crows with their grey napes as a wretched assembly, all shouting lies to one another. In their dusty black coats, they resemble barristers or priests. Against the grand stucco columns, the crows are a delegation. He draws one quickly in the corner of a sketch of Tippoo's Mosque: he draws it badly, it reminds him of a sootikin. He wonders if that really had been Osman Ali on the Esplanade. His drawings of such buildings in Lucknow he thinks are better. He turns back the pages of the sketchbook and looks at a drawing of distant palaces, with onion-domes.

Giorgio has a bed in an antechamber. He seems pleased enough with the arrangement. Lear assures Young Baring that Giorgio approves of him. When Giorgio shows an interest in the catering of the grand establishment, Baring arranges a tour of the Government House kitchens, great clattering halls full of steam and flashing metal. The head chefs are called *khansamas* and they work their minions fiercely. He hears the khansamas shouting commands, bidding the men chop faster till their fingers blur against the blades. Giorgio cannot believe that the dishes being prepared are everyday English ones. As for the khansamas, Giorgio fears and respects them. The khansamas invite him to share their own meal. The khansamas are all Muslims, except one, darker than the others, who speaks Portuguese, a Roman Catholic. They all sit around a mound of chicken pilau flavoured with saffron and slivers of almond. Then they drink beakers of tea brewed with ginger, salt and dried lemon. After that Giorgio takes all his meals with the khansamas. He tells Lear how much he looks forward to dinner in the kitchens. A special feast is to be consumed on the Burra Din. '*Dove si trova la cucina?*' Lear asks him.

Lear calls out in the night. A bearer in white pyjamas appears at his bedside. He can't get back to sleep. He worries that Giorgio is in a drunken stupor. A good servant never drinks. Lear lies awake fretting about Giorgio, the man in white pyjamas and where the smell of burning is coming from.

In the morning a letter with a rolled package is delivered to Lear. The script is odd; bogus Elizabethan, red ink:

My Dear Sir –

Please forgive my incredulity. My man Osman Ali put me right & I do beg your pardon. Indeed there was a sleeping minstrel in that big tree. He came to our gate the following Thursday. I questioned him myself. I don't know if you

*know about another line—practised by Jadoos around here—
which is to call at houses where there's been a death—
bringing pictures of the deceased. Only without pupils in
their eyes. You pays them & they paints them in. Then the
deceased can see in the next life. Back to the subject of Mr
Moore. He was keen on the Jadoos himself. Another of the
things left behind was a sheaf of drawings he'd purchased
from them. I am passing these on to you as an apology for
my sharpness. Please understand that I suffer horribly with
debilitation of the gut. It puts me in a state—is the truth. As
to the pictures—I don't see any worth in native art that is
made for the lowest—but they might serve as souvenirs in
years to come. I think you could keep them or perhaps you
would return them to Mr Moore in London. Anyways—I
have no need of them. Sir—may I take this opportunity to
wish you a Happy Christmas?*

Yours truly—
William Williams Esq.
Taragunje

'Well, well, well,' says Lear.

Moore's Jadoo pictures are alarming, childish, savage. One
is of an enormous spotted cat with long needle claws, with a
caste mark on its brow, bloodshot eyes, pointed teeth and a
blood-red tongue hanging out. On his back sits a tiny man,
seen in profile, looking to Lear like an Egyptian. The tiny man
is holding a quill and a rosary. Another shows a demon king
with a dancing girl. The black-faced king wears a crown made
of leaves—along the lower edge Moore has written: *The frenzy
of the birds is of no interest to the trees.* Of some interest these
pictures, something to please children, magic paintings. Then,
for just a few seconds, Lear has much the same sensation as
one might have sitting in a stationary railway carriage when a
train on a parallel track passes the window, that false sense of
propulsion. Lear feels that he is whizzing forward. This gives

way to dark thoughts: both the demon and the morbids bring piercing shame. Lear's depression, the morbids, can be mistaken for laziness. It isn't—the bed is a rack of despair. A man is thought unhealthy who lolls in bed. The element of shame in Lear's depression flashes mercilessly. The demon, on the other hand, in full attack would mark Lear as unclean, unhealthy—a ghastly old thing to be bundled away. The demon can ruin everything. Lear gathers himself into shape and declaims, 'O sleep, thou fiend! Thou blackness of the night! How sad and frightful are these thy dreams!' Giorgio is instantly at the door. Giorgio understands. He shoos the demon as he shoos away dogs. Giorgio is there for dogs and demons. Lear feels safe just intoning his name.

ဢ 03

Christmas dinner is comparatively intimate; there are no more than thirty guests. As usual, they come in looking straight ahead, never speaking to each other unless they are already acquainted and, if they are, muttering to one another about the others. Lear feels ungainly in Society, especially when the Quality are all in their finery, he's aware of the pigment in his fingernails and the turpentine in his beard. He's no longer comfortable standing and talking to strangers though, close to, he can still charm. Lear has no need for new friendships; he is civil when spoken to but he feels ugly, deaf, badly dressed, irritable and sensitive.

People know Lear's poems in India, but nobody seems to know his paintings. Painting has been his living, never enough of one, since the age of sixteen. The 'crickets' dismiss Lear's oils as over-meticulous (to every blade of grass, its shadow) too concerned with accuracy. The Royal Academy hangs his paintings far too high. Only people on stilts may look properly. His water-colours are freer; wide horizons, receding mountains. He's instructed Her Majesty in water-colour practice. The pictures he makes for children, the sort of pictures that appear in his Books of Nonsense, he makes with ease and speed. Children love these little pictures but some adults find them ugly and half-wild. Because of the blessed poems (regardless that he's known Lord Northbrook for twenty-five years) some fellow-guests treat Lear as an entertainer hired for the festivities. He isn't disposed to play the Merry Andrew for them.

> *My jests are cracked, my coxcomb fallen, my bauble confiscated, my cap decapitated. Toll the bell; for oh! for oh! Jack Pudding is no more!*

Lady Emma, in a green bustled dress much too old for her, rustles up to Lear. He has not seen her since Lucknow.

Today she is the image of poor Elizabeth, her mother. The same voice: '*Joyeux Noel, mon cher*! We're so delighted you're with us. It's much nicer for Father to be with his old friends at Christmas.'

'It couldn't be nicer for me, my dear.'

She is a little shy with him: 'How have you been?'

'You wouldn't really want to hear. But here I am.'

'In good enough shape.'

'Do you think so?' Lear asks. There may be an undertone in the way he asks because Emma moves away from him, without answering.

The dining-room can seat over a hundred guests so they all seem rather marooned in the middle of the room, under the great Belgian chandeliers. They are served sausages, tinned salmon, prawn curry, mango fish, devilled ortolans, roast beef, spiced beef, saddle of goat, various curried vegetables and pilaffs. Then there is Christmas cake and some good old cheddar cheese, followed by nuts. The shining faces, flushed by claret and champagne, bob like apples and pigs in the candlelight.

Lear is sitting near Young Baring and a large pallid woman, Miss Lydia Spin, the middle-aged daughter of a retired

General. The General himself is not present, due to ill health. 'Involuntary running, or festination. His nerves are attacked,' says the daughter calmly. 'Of course, an old campaigner of eighty-five can't stand such a pace. It's left him exhausted, quite done in.'

'Festination?' Baring is interested.

'Ghastly for him,' Miss Spin says. 'He'll be pottering along when, all of a sudden, he breaks into a sprint.'

'And this quite involuntary?'

'Oh quite. We've been dispatched two Jats to walk behind. Big strong chaps. If Daddy looks about to bolt, they hook an arm each. Of course, his legs do thrash about but he stays in the right place.'

'Do horses suffer from festination?' asks Lear.

'They do when I'm astride 'em. Start off slowly, then up goes the pace. Next thing, it's galloping. From now on, I shall ask for a horse that doesn't festinate.'

'You must ask for two stout syces to walk beside you.'

'Four. One for each leg.'

'Oh, I do like to trot a little,' twinkles Lear, 'canter up hillsides...'

He asks Miss Spin: 'Do you live in Calcutta?'

'Goodness, no. We're staying here as well. In a different wing.'

'So your father's resting upstairs.'

'Yes, poor thing. He loves Christmas. We live in the mofussil.'

'What does that mean? I keep hearing the word.'

'It means nowhere in particular, up country, somewhere.'

'But where in particular is your mofussil?'

'Well, we're not so far away. Gorumara. A journey of three days or so.'

'Is it mountainous there?'

'Well, it's the terai of course. Hilly, jungly. Daddy passed through it once on a campaign. Knew at a flash it was where he wanted to live...'

'How romantic...'

'Well, it is heavenly. But we're leaving, you see. I shall miss it. I hardly know what England will be like.'

Lear cannot begin to describe England.

Lord Northbrook has an amusing beard. It starts as a tuft on his chin, then grows down the front of his neck, leaving his face hairless. It is healthy, thick and dark brown. In a high collar, the Viceroy's beard resembles a mink trim. In a plain collar, it as if he has a slim young cat sleeping around his neck, which pleases Lear who likes cats immensely. But, try as he might, Lear can't sparkle.

Lydia Spin asks, 'Where were you at school, Mr Lear?'

'I was not, ma'am.'

His sketching stool has lately collapsed beneath him, by dint of which he has grazed his coccyx. It is most inflamed, catching his temper when he sits too long at dinner. Young Baring remarks, 'I notice you're hobbling a bit, old boy.'

'Well, my back, you see. And I've new boots that don't pinch my heels but squeeze my toes instead.'

'A horse stood on my foot when I was a boy,' says Baring, 'and broke my big toe. The doctor bound it to a splint and bandage. And it mended in due course. But, do you know, I can still feel the splint and the bandage, though they were removed thirty-five years ago.'

Miss Spin: 'My word, isn't that queer?'

Baring continues, 'The point of my story is that even if a shoe fits my foot like a second skin, it'll still feel too tight because of that ghostly splint.'

'I don't think my corns are spectral at all,' says Lear.

Lydia Spin says, patting Lear's arm: 'But, Mr Lear, I so wanted to tell you. Daddy knows all about Swat. Fine partridges up there. Oh, do give us *The Akond of Swat*, Mr Lear...'

In sudden exuberance, Lear stands on his chair. Baring calls for silence. Looking like a speckled owl, Lear raises his hands. His fingers are the tips of wings emerging from sleeves. He asks his listeners in a slow reedy voice: 'Who, or why, or which, or what, is the Akond of Swat?' All the shining faces sit back, preparing to shout the responses. Soon they are all laughing. Lear, who has loathed most of them until this moment, experiences a surge of benevolence towards all gathered around him.

'Does he study the wants of his own dominion? Or doesn't he care for public opinion...'

'A JOT! The Akond of Swat?' shouts Baring and those around him.

'To amuse his mind do people show him pictures, or anyone's last new poem...'

'Or WHAT, for the Akond of Swat?' cries young Lady Emma and those around her.

'At night if he suddenly screams and wakes, do they bring him only a few small cakes?'

'Or a LOT, for the Akond of Swat?' booms the Viceroy of India and his entire Christmas party.

'Eshwat!' laugh the servants in the corridors. Everybody cheers at the end. Up soars Lear's spirit in an ecstasy of acceptance.

Later on Baring fetches from his study a book to show Lear. It is *A Description of Bengal* by Lady Dorcas Vaughan, published by MacNab of Edinburgh in 1869. The passage he has found describes Bhavani Place:

The southern and eastern parts of Bhavani District, bounded by the Padma and crossed by the smaller rivers Bhavani and Brahmani, conform to the familiar topography of eastern Bengal. Low, alluvial, immensely fertile and quite densely populated, it is a landscape of fields and paddies so vividly green that the colour seems to stain the lower reaches of the sky above them. Its inhabitants (thought slippery, amphibious in their habits by

*the officials) travel by country boat or swim from village to
village. In the monsoon these lands are inundated. When
the land drains, it yields abundant crops of jute, rice, fruit
and vegetables.*

*The northern and western parts of Bhavani District are
raised some forty or fifty feet above the level of the
cultivated land, a tableland intersected by ridges and
winding depressions. The land in these depressions is called*
baid, *and is used for crops; otherwise the upland is forested
and the occupation of its inhabitants is gathering leaves
and sticks. The inhabitants of this upland are called*
Banua, *meaning wild or 'of the forest'–they are shunned
by the cultivators. The British, tiring of the level and
shimmering paddies, find the upland picturesque with its
rolling slopes and leafy shades. There are tigers among the
gajari trees. The British come to hunt, as guests of the
land's owners, the Dey family of Barapukur, in whose
zamindari much of Bhavani District falls. There are
cottages in the woods. The Deys' residence, Bhavani Place,
was built in 1846. A residence called Place is unusual in
Bengal and many take it to be a misspelling of Palace. The
choice was in fact influenced by the names of houses in our
English novels. The local people call it the Rajbari. It is a
classical villa, a* phoolbari *or flower house. The gardens
that surround the house are elaborate, with espaliers and
parterres and a series of cut ponds, perfectly square.*

Lear bids goodnight to Lord Northbrook, who is standing with
Lady Emma in the corridor. The Viceroy of India clasps the
landscape painter's shoulders and tells him he is an old and
honoured friend. Lear beams at the Viceroy's daughter. 'You
are so like your Mama,' he says.

Emma's face drops: 'Please. I so wish you'd stop saying that.'

In his rooms, Lear plunges back into despondence. To stem
his anxiety, he sorts through his equipment. Giorgio helps

pack the boxes of crayons, pigments, blades and brushes that he now deems unnecessary for the continuation of his tour. They put the boxes into a yellow-covered trunk that Lear bought in Alexandria. Into the trunk go Moore's Jadoo pictures. The trunk is sealed to be dispatched the next day to Bombay, thence to Italy.

He lies in bed, thinking of London parks. There she is, about a hundred yards away, his sister Ann, standing quite still on the shining grass beside the cherry trees, looking away over the common that is flooded with afternoon sunlight. Lear can't approach her. She starts to walk with her arms lightly outstretched along the line of cherry trees, her head bent slightly forward. Lear feels that the whole landscape is streaming outwards from her arms, streaming into them and out along them, and her presence seems to dilate and expand as though she controls his breathing. Lear is aware that his brain is working, anchoring his behaviour, but (that different thing) his mind is weaving arabesques—like blue smoke curling towards a lamp—he finds himself, by oblique processes, helpless, hopeless.

A diffuse internal excitement, initially slight then developing in volume—yet the source is imperceptible. It's not a single thing at all. It's not a noise, a light, an obsessive thought, nor anything of the kind.

Whatever it is, it can become an enormous number of things—a blurred augmentation, a presence, a crowd. Lear senses a vibration, a faint murmur which never sharpens enough to be audible, a quivering danger, making faint recriminations. Always this infinitesimal agitation, this vibrating metal plate.

When Lear was a small boy, there was another Lear family, to whom they were not related but great friends, who lived at Arundel. According to the story, Lear's father, walking in the City of London, had passed a brass plate with his own name,

Jeremiah Lear, engraved upon it. He enquired within and beheld his namesake. That was how the Jeremiah Lears came to know each other and a long affection grew between the families based upon this coincidence.

Sometimes, the Bowman's Lodge Lears visited the Batworth Park Lears. How orderly life in Sussex had seemed to him—the low hills and wandering streams.

The first time they visited, he climbed a tree to pick a gage. The gages had transparent skins, pretty, like plums already peeled on the trees, and because one seldom peels a plum, fascinating. He slipped off to the orchard while the others finished tea. He wasn't a good climber but there was a ladder and the branches looked strong. There were nets suspended between the trees to catch the fruit. He climbed the ladder and crawled along a branch. That instantly broke!

Lear landed in the fruit net that stopped his fall but gave way beneath his weight, leaving him tangled on the grass, with a bash on his head and squashed fruit all over his clothes. The indignity of his predicament set the orchard lurching and swimming around him. He struggled to free himself from the net, but it was as if the demon was in the net with him, pulling the mesh tight across Lear's mouth and poking his fingers up Lear's nose. Lear had writhed and spluttered until Ann came running through the kitchen garden. She sat beside him and spoke in a gentle scolding voice, telling him to pull through, to remember Jesus, while all the time he buckled and thrashed. Two gardeners came to help unwind him.

And then he remembers waking in a cool striped room, without Ann but with another sister, Harriett, beside the sofa.

And this demon oppressed me then 'I not knowing' its worry & misery. Every morning in the little study while learning my lessons—: all day long: & always in the evening & at night. Nor could I have been more than 6 I think—for I remember whole years before I went to school— at 11. The strong will of sister Harriett put a short pause to the misery—but very short. How well I remember that evening!

On Boxing Day morning. Lear decides against plein-air. Giorgio sleeps while his master scratches at a board.

Not over well. Worked at colour, but very badly, with new tube colours as worry me. Nor was the morning clear. However, it don't make much difference I think, for I doubt being able to do this view at all. Sun very hot, wind very cold: worried and depressed.

ജ ൦ഭ

Giorgio complains of a stiff neck. He can behave like a mule. Lear sets off alone to Burrapoker Street.

The landau passes through the gates of Government House and joins the northward traffic. Lear, accustomed already to rougher roads and tongas, sits cautiously in the carriage with one hand holding the vehicle's side as if, at any moment, he might be flung out. The landau is as far from a tonga as any conveyance in Calcutta could be; it is sprung and oiled, the pair of horses that pull it are fit and gleaming and the coachmen dressed in immaculate livery. The conveyance belongs, after all, to the Viceroy of India. Lear feels a little shabby in it, embarrassed by the stares he receives. As a viceregal guest he necessarily draws attention. Most of those who lift their hats do so merely to wish him well but Lear still senses their disapproval. The reluctant cynosure blinks behind his gold spectacles and pulls the brim of his hat down. When self-conscious, he fiddles with the grey beard that hangs over his chest like a bib. The scotoma in his eye is particularly fizzy, pulling entire aspects of Calcutta into its effervescent depths.

Burrapoker Street is in the Sutanuti area of Calcutta, the Black Town as called. The traffic the landau joins consists of countless pedestrians, equestrians, broughams, barouches, governess-carts, hackneys, hackeries, garries, tongas, pack-mules and camels. Lear watches a goatherd drive his flock straight through the wheeling chaos and then two men running with a small brown bear hanging upside down from a long pole; the poor beast's paws are bound together, as are its jaws from which come muffled shrieks. A water-carrier, with two bags hanging like lungs from a yoke, trots alongside Lear's carriage. The air smells to Lear suddenly of burning lemon leaves. The streets the carriage passes through remind Lear of London but a London of iridescent stucco, with a circus emptied into it. The noise is rhythmic, almost percussive: footfalls, hoofbeats and shouts, interspersed with bursts of discordant music and sounds like the rending of cloth. For a few minutes a marching band accompanies Lear playing *Happy Birthday to You*. The blaring gaiety only saddens him; he turns to observe a dancing monkey (dressed, like the bandsmen, in a stiff scarlet jacket) and when he looks back the band has been replaced by a procession of mendicants ringing bells and blowing through conch shells, chanting about Shankar and Shiva. One of the mendicants is a dwarf.

The air dances with dust, motes, mites and unidentifiable flies. The air of Manchester in high summer, thinks Lear. The landau clips on towards Chitpore Road where all the shops are overstuffed, their goods spilling over the pavements into the road. In this quarter the buildings remind Lear of modern Rome, but many are shoddy and collapsing at the corners. Much of the trade is in cloth: piece-goods, cambays, chintzes and mulmuls hanging on pegs and piled on trestles. Lear notices a wig shop, or perhaps a horsehair shop, several shops selling ornate hookahs, a shop that displays nothing but velvet caps. Lear sees bewildering fruit arranged in bright pyramids. There is a bird market with caged mynahs and jackdaws. He sees leopard cubs in cages (either leopards or large spotted cats) but when he tries to look back at them, the crowd hides the cages.

Shyamali informs Dey that a large bird has been flying over the women's quarters, swooping at jewellery. She explains to her husband that it is a bird that none of the women have seen before in Bengal. It is not a crow, but by common consent more like a crow than a kite and it is covered in greenish-black feathers. Dey is eager to identify this bird. His wife scolds him: 'No! It hasn't come back. Don't we all have eyes? We will tell you when it next appears.'

Now Dey is in a bad mood. His cousin's children cluster about his chair, whining. They want a story but he has not finished his lunch. He complains there are too many shadows. He longs to look out over fields of mustard blossom. He believes the yellow improves his eyesight. When he speaks to the children, Dey's voice is deep and ponderous. He tells them about a meal Gouri cooked for Lord Shiva, that started with aubergine and finished with spinach and sour plums. There were twenty dishes in all and Dey names each one. The children listen politely but show little interest.

'No fish,' remarks the children's father, Dey's cousin Jagadish, emerging into the light. 'I would have asked for fish.'

It was written down three centuries ago, Dey tells them, by the *Kabikankan Mukandaram*. The children rock on their heels and say nothing. Dey often throws references to poets like Kashidas or Jayadeva into his conversation.

Jagadish calls for some sandesh. 'Look at all these children,' he tells the servant, as if there are more than three of them, 'they need fattening'. When the sandesh arrives, Jagadish takes the marble plate and crumbles the sweets into tiny pieces. He eats most of the pieces himself.

In the eighteenth century Calcutta's merchant-princes dressed like nawabs from Lucknow. A century later, Dey still dresses in the Persian manner but closer inspection shows his taste to be more Bangla, less Avadhi. His shirts are of Dacca muslin, his chapkans and chogas of Murshidabad silk, his balaposh shawls from Berhampore, his pointy slippers made of jute or kid.

Jagadish, by contrast, dresses in the phool-babu style lampooned by the Kalighat painters: a tight black jacket with a white tuberose buttonhole, a dhoti from Farasdanga, black patent leather boots. Jagadish's hairstyle is based upon that of the late Prince Albert, his moustache is waxed and he carries a silver-tipped swagger stick. Sometimes he wears a sash across his chest.

Dey mocks his cousin for dressing like a fop. Jagadish retorts that Dey is a Hindu dressed as a Mussulman.

Bechu, the adolescent son of another cousin, joins the party. He touches Dey's feet, then his own forehead, with his right hand. Dey has high hopes for Bechu who already displays some literary taste. Dey asks Bechu to recite the verses he has been practising. In a prancing voice, perhaps to distinguish the words from his own, Bechu begins:

'Mahadevi, wife of Lord Shiva,

Daughter of the mighty Himalayas...'

Jagadish snaps at the boy: 'There's no need to spit.'

'Let him continue,' says Dey.

Bechu recites for several minutes without interruption, bringing the verse to a close with the lines:

'She is Uma, whose beauty shines,

Gouri the brilliant yellow,

Parvati the mountaineer

And Hemavati the mountain;

She is Jagan Mata, the mother of the world.'

Jagadish and his children clap. 'Uncle Balendra himself could not have recited that so well.'

Bechu says, 'Balendra-Uncle wrote it.'

'Balendra would have sung the words. It is a song,' says Dey. Bechu excuses himself by saying that he learned the words from Balendra's notebooks, nobody taught him the music. His voice is whiny again.

Jagadish disappears into one of the rooms and comes back with a rosewood casket. As soon as his children see the box, they squeal with delight. Inside the box is a toy cobra fashioned from stiff wires covered in green chintz. At the side of the box is a brass lever in a slot.

Jagadish instructs Bechu to put his finger in the snake's mouth.

'Come, Bechu. It's only a puppet.'

The boy shrugs and does as he is told. Jagadish pulls the lever back and a sharp jolt of electricity runs up Bechu's arm through his finger.

Bechu cries out.

Jagadish releases the lever and the pain stops.

Everybody, including Dey, roars with laughter.

'You see,' splutters Jagadish, 'it bit you'.

Bechu's young cousins cackle, bent double with mirth.

Jagadish claps his hands and a man comes in playing a shehnai. The surprise makes Dey smile. In comes another musician playing a drum. Dey stops smiling and sends both musicians away.

Jagadish looks crestfallen. He had intended the musicians to raise Dey's spirits. Shyamali and the scholars had advised him that Dey was despondent; Jagadish feels it his duty to lighten things.

The servant leaves Lear in a reception room looking at the pictures hanging in three rows along the walls. Some are by artists Lear knows, pieces they might shudder to see again. Lear, in his apprehensive state, is disheartened to see so many mistakes on display. It is almost an exhibition of failed effects, wobbliness and the British inability to see a landscape. He holds his hat in front of him, rotating it slowly. On a heavy side-table stands a zograscope, a turned wooden stand supporting a hinged mirror and lens, which may be used to view an image placed beside the stand, the optical properties of the lens giving the image an effect of depth and perspective. It is quite an antique—Lear had amused himself as a child with a zograscope at Batworth Park.

A man with a waxed moustache, wearing a tight black coat and a pleated muslin skirt, comes in. He looks to Lear like a clergyman. 'Your Highness?'

The man replies in English with nasal Cockney inflections: 'I'm Jagadish Dey. His Highness is my cousin, Pannalal Chandranath Dey. He's waiting, actually. Please come...'

Lear follows him, sheepishly, noticing the churchy smell of incense and the click of Jagadish's heels on the marble lozenges. Jagadish has been asked to attend this meeting because Dey wants him to devise a further entertainment, a fête in Lear's honour. A Nautch in the Grand Manner, the sort of mehfil Matilal gave. Lear likes all the marble, how cool it must keep the place. Then he is in another courtyard, blinking for it is flooded with light, and a tall man, dressed in a patterned silk coat and a shawl, looms towards him. Lear notes the green eyes and the red mouth. 'Your Highness?'

Dey nods. 'Mr Lear. Sit down, won't you please? Do you fancy a cup of tea? Perhaps a sherbet? Do you like sherbet?'

'Yes, please. I mean sherbet, not tea. Thank you.'

There is a small gathering. Relatives mostly, Lear understands, and a dark-skinned middle-aged gent looking distinguished in an English morning suit. His name is Mr Dutt—he has just returned from four years in England, the last eighteen months in Cambridge. 'I wanted my girls to attend some lectures.'

'His girls are the cleverest in Calcutta,' says Jagadish.

'My wife is especially fond of Toru,' says Dey.

Mr Dutt says, 'Your dear wife has given her so many books...'

'We have plenty...'

'My daughter is talking with Her Highness this minute but she will join us. She knows your poetry, Mr Lear.' Lear is modestly flattered.

'She speaks and writes in French and German,' says Jagadish.

Lear asks, 'And when you say *girl*?'

'Seventeen. She translates French poetry into English...'

'I say!'

Mr Dutt says, 'She is a Christian, Mr Lear. Ours is a Christian family.'

Dey says, 'Whereas my family are devotees of the Great Mother,' and the crimson tip of his tongue pokes between his black lips.

'Oh,' says Lear. The Raja's manner resembles an actor's— he almost seems to be wearing make-up. It puzzles Lear that he too speaks English with a London accent. It is almost an echo of his own voice. Has there been a London governess in the family? He's read of such arrangements. A woman like one of his own sisters would account for such a voice.

A white marble beaker appears, containing a cold viscous liquid, a sweet floral soup. 'It's rather exotic,' says Lear tactfully.

'Muchkund petals. They soothe headaches.'

'How did you know?' Lear is surprised. 'Do I look peevish?'

Dey smiles, 'I'm afraid I have been peevish. But, don't worry, I've already had my sherbet.' The meeting passes in informality: an extremely generous fee for an oil painting and several drawings is offered, accepted and never mentioned again. Lear had expected a diffident encounter but instead there are iced drinks and small talk. The atmosphere seems theatrical to Lear, the Palace a battered old set, the props a bit bashed, the entourage Cockney players, King Pannalal the actor-manager. Lear is comfortable among them, it is all agreeable. Lear asks, 'Are you vegetarian, Your Highness?'

Dey replies, 'I eat mutton sometimes. I prefer vegetable preparations. I am not vegetarian, but many of my scholars are. My wife has never tasted meat, yet she eats *rui* fish with gusto.'

Lear: 'What is a rooey fish?'

Mr Dutt: 'It is a species of carp—or is it perch?'

Jagadish says: 'My cousin does not enjoy our Calcutta sweets.'

Dey snaps, 'I find the craving for sweetmeats childish.'

Lear says that too much sugar can make his head ache; the same with champagne.

They are joined by Mr Dutt's clever daughter: a bright-faced girl, small for seventeen, an Indian version of Rossetti's *Beata Beatrix* with jaw out-thrust and long black hair thrown behind her in waves, dressed in artistic Pre-Raphaelite clothes made of patterned Bengal cottons. At her collar is a moonstone brooch as big as a duck's egg. The youth called Bechu says something to her in Bangla, whatever she says in reply stings him. She makes straight for Lear and after some light exchange—she tells Lear she prefers France to England though she was only there four months and Lear tells her he suffers in the English climate—Miss Dutt tells Lear that she regards his poetry highly but finds his verses so sad. 'Oh no no,' says Lear, as if talking to a child because of her size, 'they are not true, you see. They're Nonsense...'

Mr Dutt tells Lear that he too has read the *Book of Nonsense*. He says there is something similar in Bengali folk-songs. 'The singer uses outlandish imagery in riddles. The listener makes his own sense of it. He has to find the hidden sense behind the songs.'

Lear says, 'I may assure you there is no hidden sense behind mine.'

Toru Dutt: 'If they weren't translated into this world of your Nonsense, they would be desolate...'

Mr Dutt smiles, 'I see Toru is worried about the state of your soul...'

'Do not belittle me, Father. I am small enough as it is. I do believe I've been shrinking ever since our return. But, Mr Lear, why are you so despondent? My sister believes all English poetry is despondent. We prefer to read French.'

Jagadish steps in, just as Lear is beginning to feel uncomfortable. 'Mr Lear, come and meet the children.' Lear follows him along a cool shadowy corridor, decorated with Hindu gods and Roman generals, to the nursery where a maid bows and says the children are resting. 'Then we shall see them later,' says Jagadish, patting Lear on the shoulder. Outside the nursery are two gilt chairs padded with striped cushions that, in their Oriental decoration, might have come from Brighton Pavilion. 'Stop,' says Jagadish, 'let us rest for a while. Please, sit down, Mr Lear.' Lear sits on one of the Oriental chairs. Within its striped cushion is a musical apparatus that is activated by pressure. The musical chair plays the *Blue Danube*. Lear is greatly amused. He stands up and the waltz stops.

Jagadish then sits on the other Oriental chair, similarly equipped, that plays the *Minute Waltz*. Lear sits again and the two waltzes strain against each other, the melodies crossing one another giddily. After a minute, the two stand up again.

On the way back, Jagadish asks, 'Shall I call for some more sweets? Do you like them, our Calcutta sweets? Do they compare to English ones?'

'Quite different, both delicious. But don't order them just for me...'

'I say, was Toru badgering you there?'

'She's a little sharp.'

'She can't help it. She might be over-educated. Her poor sister is ill. They had to come back. The cold weather was killing them.'

'Does Mr Dutt always wear English clothes?'

'No. He might have worn such clothes in England, of course. I expect he put them on for you, don't you think? Now, what about those sandesh?'

Toru Dutt is waiting for him. She springs from behind a column. 'Have you read *Poésies Barbares* by Leconte de Lisle?'

Lear is a little perplexed by the gauche little genius. He says, 'I haven't. I'm not all that clever, you see...'

'It's a pity, but I could send you some of my translations.'

'That would be kind. You could send them to Government House...'

She cuts in, 'I know, I know where you are staying. We saw your carriage.' Then, in quite a different tone of voice, she says: 'If you ask me, the greatest English poet is Lord Byron.'

Lear says, 'Oh yes. I think so too. He was my hero, when I was a small boy. I sat in the passage and cried, when Byron died.'

She smiles: 'That is verse, surely—I sat in the passage and cried, when Byron died...'" Lear sees her charm at last.

Into the room come the two bespectacled medical gentlemen from the train, the one still in his white lawn pajamas and the other still in his green waistcoat. Lear recognises them at once, but the haggard one just nods at him, as if he has been expecting to see him, while the other snubs him. 'Basu and Nagaraj work for me,' explains Dey, dismissing them with a turn of his wrist.

Lear wonders if they are personal physicians to the Raja. He asks, 'In what capacity do those two gentlemen serve you, Sir?'

'They are helping me compile my magnum opus,' says Dey, with a little smile at the phrase for Mr Dutt, who tells Lear, 'His Highness's book is called the *Purnachandroday*, the Rising Moon.'

'It's a lovely title. What is it, a book of fairy tales?'

Toru Dutt laughs, embarrassing Lear.

Dey smiles: 'Well, it does include fairy tales among many other things. I am translating a selection of passages from our Indian medical literature, much of which was written long long ago. My aim is to bring these ancient writers into our modern world. But the blessed thing grows like a plant, there is so much to include. And sometimes there is so much that needs to be explained to an English reader...'

Mr Dutt: 'His Highness has been working on this anthology for more than twenty years, Mr Lear.'

Dey says he will show Lear the passage he is working on. He sends for Basu (white lawn pajamas) who brings a sheet of paper covered in writing with various words crossed out and notes all down the margin. He explains that it is from a book by a sage called Susruta, who was concerned with winds.

'Do you mean indigestion?'

'Flatulence. That is what you call 'the wind' in English. But Susruta said there were winds whistling about inside our bodies as well. He saw nothing wrong with that. Unless the winds blow off course, then you get whirlwinds, typhoons, all kinds of ghastly things occurring inside.'

Mr Dutt nods and asks rhetorically: 'Could life continue without wind? Everything trembles, always...'

Toru Dutt: 'He makes it sound terrifying but in fact it is no more terrifying than Rabelais...'

'I've never read Rabelais.'

Mr Dutt tells Lear that Susruta, who lived in the sixth century, was a royal surgeon amongst whose talents was rhinoplasty—he could replace a nose lost in battle with a false one.

'What did it look like?' asks Lear.

'I believe the nose looked well enough,' says Mr Dutt, 'but the cheek from which it was constructed was left scarified...'

Toru Dutt: 'Oh, but much worse than a few scars to have no nose at all.'

'This represents an afternoon's endeavour,' says Dey, handing Lear the paper.

The holy wind is God, they say. It is without restraint, everlasting, everywhere. It is revered in all the worlds as the Self of all creatures. It is the cause of the existence, origination and termination of all beings, the unmanifest cause of manifestation; it is dry, cool, light and cutting. It moves horizontally, with the qualities of sound and touch, and is never still. It has unimaginable power. It is the chief humour and the king of all diseases. Quick-acting, restless, it dwells in the gut and in the anus. Wind which is not irritated maintains the balance of the humours, the tissues of the body and the digestive fire. It allows one to *apprehend the objects of sense, it allows actions to proceed smoothly. As the digestive fire divides into types, depending on name, place, action and ailment, so the wind, though one, divides as well into fore-breath (*prana*), up-breath (*udana*), mid-breath (*samana*), intra-breath (*vyana*) and down-breath (*apana*). Located in their proper places, these five breaths cause movement in all living creatures.*

The wind that passes through the mouth is called prana. Prana supports the body. It causes the food to be swallowed, and it supports breathing. Corrupted, it causes hiccoughs and wheezing. The highest of winds, that moves upwards, is udana. Udana allows excellent speech and song but also ailments above the collarbone. Samana moves in conjunction with the digestive fire through the stomach and intestines. Samana separates food into its component parts for the well-being of the body. The ailments of samana include abdominal swelling, the dying down of the digestive fire and diarrhoea. Vyana moves through the whole body, to make the juices, the sweat and the blood flow. Enraged, it causes ailments through the whole body. Apana, the down-breath, lives in the gut. At the right time, this wind draws downward the faeces and urine, semen, foetus and menstrual blood. When apana is enraged, it stings the bladder and the rectum. When samana and apana misfunction, the flow of semen and urine is stemmed. If all five breaths are irritated, the body is undone.

Lear shivers. He is strong enough today to deal with echoes, voices. At certain times, weaker in himself, any room can whistle and scream like an aviary, though only he can hear the birds.

A proposal is made that Lear should travel to Bhavani Palace with Dey and his coterie, making most of the journey by river. 'Do you like boats?' asks Dey.

'I am never happier than afloat,' says Lear, though it isn't really true.

'Then this is a most felicitous occasion, and we must prolong the pleasure. Do you like dancing girls? We shall give a Nautch in your honour,' declares Jagadish.

'I like dancing elephants,' he says, spinning his hat on his right forefinger. Already, Jagadish has such a vision of the mehfil that it can accommodate Lear's throwaway comment. 'Then we shall engage Goki-Bai who dances on a platform that is mounted on the tusks of an elephant!' He is excited.

So is Lear: 'By golly, does she really?'

'Indeed, indeed. With her musicians up on the elephant's back in a howdah.'

'What, a big brass band?'

'No, no. The sarangi player. I suppose you'd say it's akin to the violin.'

'More like the cello,' says Dey.

'And two drummers, hand drummers. We call these drums tablas.'

'Tom-toms,' says Lear.

'Indeed, indeed. We have had elephants here before...'

'Seventy years ago,' says Dey.

Then Mr Dutt opines that surely taste should reign, the ethereal strains of spiritual song would be preferable to a circus act. 'Oh, I don't mind a circus act at all,' says Lear.

Dey finds his cousin's enthusiasm distasteful. Jagadish organises the pujas throughout the year. His cousin's constant need for jollity is vulgar. Dey is never as keen on festivals as everyone else in the family is. He is pleased however to find Lear so agreeable. The poems had worried him a little. Indeed, he is relieved to find Lear sane.

9
___

*T*he Chinese streamers make the hotel rooms dance—
anxiety makes Williams dizzy. He remedies this with a
large dose of Propter's Panacea diluted with Seltzer.

In a glass vitrine, mounted on the wall, a great mahseer
floats stiffly through curious vegetation, small green roses
constructed by the taxidermist from sola pith. The fish itself—
sixty pounds and caught by his father in the year of his death—
has a baneful canine expression, a bleary eye and a sharp
disdainful snout. Its long tight body is the colour of brass at the
sides and iron along the back, with bright orange fins.
Williams sits and writes:

> *Williams Hotel*
> *Taragunje*
>
> *December the 27th*

My Dear Sir—

*May I thank you firstly for your kind present of seeds &
your* Nonsense Songs & Stories *which I have given to the
children. They read well & should enjoy the poems—many
of which I see are quite short in length. Is that a good thing
in Poetry? I should think it is for you will get more poems in*

your time reading & if they are funny—as yours are—more mirth too. But I am not a poetical man & the subject of this letter isn't Poetry. The rest of this letter is in hope that you are well & rested & disposed to give a letter from a man you have met but once your fair & timely consideration. Please allow me to unburden myself to you—& pray do not see this as any kind of familiarity I am assuming on my part—except that you are the only other person I know with some foreknowledge of Mr Slingsby Moore. I suspect you are more likely to meet him again than I am & I am beseeching you not to accept any opinion Moore should give you about myself or Mrs Williams. Indeed I am most vexed by what this man might say—I cannot sleep.

Can you believe Sir I have been personally agitated by this man yet again? Truly—it beggars belief that he should even have returned to this hotel on the Night Before Christmas—so how could I turn him away?

Indeed Moore had money—plenty of money I saw with my own eyes—& not only did he settle the matter outstanding but agreed to pay in advance this time for my hospitality—so how could I refuse him? I am ashamed to report there were no other guests. The truth is times have been hard of late & I cannot tell you why. The place is clean—I may assure you. All our water comes from a bore-well as old as I am. It has preserved me all the time I have lived here & my dear wife & the blessed children.

I suspect the plunge in business is more to do with the new timetables; there is now no need to break one's journey except perhaps for sightseeing & apart from professional artists like your good self—who would find sights to see here? Why—there are prettier spots in Bengal to breathe the air there is no denying.

For what it's worth—there are insubstantialated rumours about my own state of health. My health—Mr Lear—is as you saw it to be. I am not an adherent of gossip—& do not believe there is always truth in it but I know how things go in Bengal.

Would you call me an infectious man? What I am is enfeebled—but this is nothing another can catch from me. I am enfeebled by my bowels—that is the sum of it—& from this enfeeblement comes a legion of parallel torments—one causing the other within—so to put it. I say again—I am not infectious.

But all that is by the by & has no bearing on Moore & his outrageous behaviour over the Festive Period. Other years Christmastide has been a big tamasha here—but this time without guests there was to be neither turkey nor peacock— instead I had a good size black pig killed—& gave most of the meat to the servants—excepting of course the Mussulman staff most of whom being in positions of higher responsibility are given cash-presentations as is more appropriate—though I have known some of them take the pork anyway calling it English Mutton. In this house we do not have a tree but instead we decorate a bow from a tree that is called Child's Life & the local people call this tree Putranjiva. *Inside the fruit there's a hard seed that they string into necklaces which they hang about the necks of sickly children to ward off illness. I do believe it is that belief that gives the tree its name & not a Christian story at all—nevertheless it is a family tradition. Moore commented on this—declaring it unusual. He seemed to find much about our lives unusual. He stared so much the children became scared of him.*

His voice would range from bat-pitch squeak to a tragic bellow & you never knew what to expect so it was 'What? What? Speak up—Mr Moore' or it was 'Pray do not shout at us—Mr Moore' & nothing in between—& so we shared our dinner like good Christians on Christmas Eve with a man hard to feel kindness toward & he himself without a shred or scrap of kindness toward us.

The bee buzzes around the flower to tell the flower that it is a flower—that is my translation from a proverb the servants use—it doesn't really mean much in English. We had chops & gravy for dinner & I must say Moore fell on the food like a beast—his whole shirt front quite covered in grease. He discomfited Mrs Williams by staring at her. I said to him—'Avert your stare Sir.' I think his game was to discomfit her so much she would be bound to speak—she does not as you may remember & this is universally accepted as her indisposition—though for convenience in short incidents I explain she does not speak English. I would be surprised—Mr Lear— if you might not indeed have asked yourself—whence does this lady hail? Is it Spain—Dalmatia or Illyria? I shall tell you—she was born in Calcutta. Do I surprise you? Is she not—in all save her olive complexion—the very essence of uxorial goodness?

This paragon rose & left the room—& she was sobbing. I shouted at him—'You will not sit at my table if you stare so at My Wife—Mr Moore!'

He answered—with such coldness as I still can feel— with these words—'You have cut out her tongue!'

But it was me what was cut for never has anyone accused me of that crime.

Let me tell you the truth Sir—Mrs Williams must have been born to or acquired by a tribe of beggars—for as an infant her tongue was removed. The Sisters found her at the age of five & housed & schooled & trained her in our Christian manners &—when she was ten—they packed her off from Calcutta to their school at Taragunje—from where at seventeen she progressed to become my dear Mother's servant & I was a young man &—I'm never sure if the old man was joshing me or not—my Father said 'The silent one keeps her charm best.' Mrs Williams has—Mr Lear—oh she has!—for me. Though it is true that—upon his very dying bed my poor father—much deluded & no doubt dazzled by the Approaching Bliss—muttered about the mistake I had made. Until then my father seemed to love her—so I was surprised. His line was that my children would be scorned as Half-Castes. But they passed as Welsh enough to him before & therefore British—for there are Welshmen with a blackness to their countenance as you will know & should I gather my family to return & live among the sheep in the mountains—why—there would be other children darker. Their mother's silence means their English is learned unbroken. I have loved my Dark Lady as much as any Fair Lady from Beaumaris as my own Mother was.

(I do not know if you have been with a dying parent yourself—Mr Lear—but it is common for them to purge themselves of foul things & bitternesses & he made other dreadful confessions so vile as to be unbelievable & often I could not stand to listen to his foul utterances)

How the brute Moore had come to that supposition I do not care to think! I pulled myself together & responded— 'Mr Moore—you have seen fit to comment upon my Wife's particular infirmity but you have no right to accuse me of performing the mutilation...'

Moore cut me short—'Do not voices trouble you? I have seen the battles you have in your sleep—remember!'

'How may you know my dreams?'

'I do not know them, but I have seen what can happen when a man cannot bear the voices any longer.'

I ignored this line of his—though it troubled me. I said 'In fact—Mr Moore—her tongue was removed in her infancy before she came into this world of Christian charity.' Those were my words to him—but I do not think he believed me because he believed himself so correct in his reading of the situation. He would not retract. Misbelief of this kind is very dangerous. If he chooses to bandy his opinions & such a man spreads false rumour by nature—why he could tarnish my name as far as it is known! I am so weak (or rather I used to be) that if my mind should coincide with another's—I would immediately be subjugated and swallowed up by him—deferential to him—but now I keep my eye on it—I'm attentive—dogged rather—at being my own master.

On the morning of the Burra Din—as you have no doubt heard it called in these parts—long before breakfast—I stood at my door & saw the most extraordinary thing: a Wave Through Gravel. What caused it—I don't know. A small earthquake perhaps. Localised. Anyway I stood atop the red steps & watched it come up the path. It was as if every piece of gravel in that path upped & rolled over. It had a bristling look & made its crunching sound. It looked like a great serpent too & when it reached the red steps it just stopped & spat a few stones upward. I have never seen the like in all my years in Taragunje. To the heathen—it would have seemed a portent—I'm sure—but I do not look for signs at all—I take things as they come—for what they are & this may sound abrasive to you—Mr Lear—for I do not know your view at all—but I do not think it is in God's interest to give us signs—instead for us to take things as they come in This Life.

Moore came with us to the Roman Church in Taragunje. I did not enquire as to whether he was RC—he asked to accompany us. You may be surprised that a Welsh family is RC but I shall tell you it was a Conversion that my father devised—& more from the absence of any Chapel in the district & his Cambrian antipathy to the Church of England—than from intense conviction—still I was educated by the Sisters & grateful I am to them—& it was through the Sisters I found my good Wife. But to be truthful—I am no longer a religious man—nor do I ever think I was much of one—writing truthfully.

I was too proud to ask Moore to retract his accusation. Instead I gave my words to him as we left the churchyard— 'You must find alternative accommodation—Mr Moore. For you have insulted my honour & the honour of my family.' Threw him OUT without dinner. But now I am agitated—

& this is why I am writing this to you Sir—because I have come to know some artistic people & some are fine men—especially photographers I would say who are partly sappers—but most are alike in drink and given to wild talk—& who in a state of spirits doesn't love a horrid tale? If this tale—which was never true—should spread through India which is common in the hotel trade—I shall be undone. Please in your kindness—scotch this rumour on my behalf—& rebuke Moore—upbraid him for bearing false witness. Do this for me please.

Yours truly,
William Williams Esq.

P.S. Should you perchance ever hear the subject of my Wife's tongue discussed abroad I trust—as a Gentleman—you will support me by telling the Truth.

Williams addresses the envelope to Lear at Government House. Then he walks out onto the verandah. Still holding the letter, he descends to the garden, grey, black and silver in the light of half the moon. He follows the gravel path to the orchard. For a minute or two Williams stands irresolute, facing the dark trees. He senses an inhalation of breath, as if the creatures are watching him in expectation. He fancies he hears them, he can sense their skittering movement, but he cannot see them in the darkness. The monkeys are not running from him but creeping towards him, necks stretched in curiosity. 'This is nonsense,' he says aloud to himself and turns back to the hotel. As he turns, he has a sensation of thin hands reaching for his back. A throng of angry, invisible monkeys seem to be pouring down from the trees, uttering simian imprecations. This horrid sense of being followed (yet if he turns there is nothing there) takes absolute possession of Williams' thoughts. He reaches the verandah, where he looks around with a painful realisation of the fragility of his mind. 'A precious fool,' he mutters, 'what a precious fool I am...'

The black trees thrash as if storm-blown, but there is no wind—outlines bristle and break apart—loud inhuman chattering—the trees are thick with monkeys. Shrieking, sniffing, spitting: the clacking of tongues and the clacking of teeth. It is his hotel, it has his name on the sign. Let anyone challenge him. Williams walks into the hall and, for a moment, flails his arms against invisible assailants. 'I shall sleep in my own time,' he warns them. Then he sits down in the hall muttering that he may never sleep again.

His father's death had been slow; for days he lay propped by a bolster in his bed, uttering (in Welsh as often as English) strange and uncharacteristic revelations, losing all his taciturnity. At the bedside, Williams felt awkward. The old man's mouth would stretch down at the sides and sometimes no utterance came but a sound like dry beans in a metal beaker; he would lift one trembling hand as if preaching. Once he told his son about a garden festooned with hanging blossoms. There he had walked among great sarus-cranes, as tall as men, with blood-red plumage on their heads and necks—when the sarus-cranes sang they had deep masculine voices, and they sang Welsh hymns like a choir. Williams had no idea how he was meant to respond to this so he had said nothing but his silence just spurred the old man to say more. The sarus-cranes had given way to reminiscences of a carnal nature. A white goat came rearing out of his father's bed. Williams couldn't bear to look at it, one glimpse of its horns and yellow eyes was enough to disgust him. It was bad enough to smell the goat. He'd covered his eyes while it skittered over the polished floor and cackled of mountings and rampings and fallings off, one woman after another, hundreds over the years. The goat, in its sly boastful voice, spoke of native women, a procession of servant-girls, listing their names. Williams had left the room before he could hear her name. A terrible possibility smoulders and sizzles within him that no Madeira, no Propter's Panacea can dowse. To think of his wife brings him nausea—when he thinks of his children (*his* children?) Williams emits a long vulpine groan.

Beneath the weight and the crush, there would not be a swarm of monkeys but one monstrous monkey made of hundreds of claws and teeth that tear and rend skin like fruit-rind. Small white bones go as tense as rods with destructive energy. Blood not liquid but a cascade of needles. Williams' own body would not be bones but blades.

Silver appears. Absolute Silver. Silver beyond all silveriness. Silver that is the beginning of Silver. Silver that triumphs through total eradication of all colours. Irrational, angry silver, swarming with lights. Frenzied, furious, riddling the retina. Horrible electric Silver, implacable, murderous. Silver in bursts and fireworks of Silver. The God of Silver. No, not a god, a howling monkey.

10

_____

_L_ ear wakes up gasping. The enormous bedroom echoes
with sounds from outside: the grinding of a wheel,
hammering, the sounds the clearer for the early morning hush.
Why are they at work so early? The sound of the hammer
brings memories of his father. Lear recalls Jeremiah not as the
greybeard at Gravesend but in his stock-broking prime. To
celebrate the Coronation in 1820, Jeremiah had a miniature
blacksmith's forge set up in a room at the top of the house in
Holloway; it became his passion. There he would evade his
duties and obligations, banging metal rods upon his anvil. He
made hooks, trivets and fire-irons. These he sometimes
presented to his frustrated clients—'All very well, but where is
our money?' Lear recalls the shining jowls and the pumping
arm; the exhaustion and excitement in his father's eyes as he
struck the metal for hours on end. Were there people, waving
sheets of paper, at the door? You couldn't hear a thing over
the hammering.

He checks the time, half past six, waits and waits but the tea
does not come. There must have been a misunderstanding.
Could someone have told the servants not to wake him? Who
would do such a thing? Young Baring? Emma?

As Lear washes, he speaks to his reflection: 'Poor Father.'

Once his father took a bag of stale muffins to the shingle
beach. 'Come on, you big white birds,' shouted Jeremiah, as if

he hadn't known they were called gulls. All they could see were grey fledglings among the cottage chimney pots, unable as yet to fly. Lear had looked at the white muffins strewn over the pebbles; he had strayed so far from his normal existence that he might have been walking on the moon. Later on it rained, but no gulls came, nobody picked the muffins up. He untangles his beard with a brush he bought in Leghorn. Then he rouses Giorgio.

The breakfast room is tall and airy, with all the punkahs swishing like sails, as if the room is bowling on an ocean breeze.

He is greeted by Miss Spin, fittingly dressed in navy blue with white trim, made by the darzi of course, for the voyage home.

He is introduced to her aged father, General Spin, a skeleton in a suit of green linen cloth, with a frightful death-mask of a face—only one eye and that a rolling veinous thing that pierces Lear to his spine.

He appears to have been eroded by salt. To Lear's surprise, General Spin's hand is a vigorous claw in a leather glove. Lear is jolted by the bony grip. The eye holds him, pulls him. 'You're the comical poet, ain't you? Demmed funny, I'm told.' In the background, watching the General's every move, are two enormous soldiers in red turbans. Lear thanks the old cadaver, the skin on whose face is the colour and texture of sliced mountain ham.

Lydia Spin pats Lear's arm. 'Daddy's supposed to be deaf, but we don't think he is.'

'Has your father tried an ear trumpet?'

'Couldn't get along with it, could you, Daddy?'

'Not at all,' says the old ghoul, 'useless article'. Turning to Lear and grabbing at his shoulder, he announces: 'I always say the human body is a bally inefficient arrangement. Instead of a mouth and a backside, why don't we have one all-purpose hole to eat and eliminate, what? We could stitch up the nose and mouth, remove the demmed stomach and all those lengths of gut—much too long, better a short ivory tube—drill an air passage, directly into the demmed lungs. The fittings would all be cut from ivory. Perfectly clean, and of mammalian origin...'

'And when you say "we"? Who exactly is going to perform such a modification?'

'I'd like to think our Army Surgeons would be capable.'

The poor old gent, thinks Lear.

Lydia Spin: 'You must understand that my father can be a little, um, miraculous. He is likely to tell you queer tales of a medical nature—that he has lived for a long time without a stomach, without intestines, almost without lungs, with a torn oesophagus, without a bladder, and with shattered ribs, he sometimes swallows parts of his own larynx with his food. But divine miracles—he calls them God's Rays—always restore what has been destroyed...'

General Spin interrupts: 'By the time my own dear wife passed away she no longer had a brain or nerves or chest or stomach or guts. All she had left was the skin and bones of a disorganised body—that was her own description of herself, her very own words—as she was dying in Gorumara...'

Miss Spin takes Lear aside while her father takes his seat: 'That's not true about Mama, by the by. She died of peritonitis.'

Lear finds the made dishes (devilled kidneys, fish balls) unappetising. 'I shall have two hard-boiled eggs and dry toast.'

Lady Emma joins them. She is so pretty in chessboard silks. It is clear that Lydia Spin finds her bumptious. Emma touches the back of Lear's hand and tells him he looks pale. 'You should eat something steadying.' Lear wants to ask her what she knows of steadying, but it would sound bad-tempered and besides some girls her age do nothing but swoon and fall over.

Miss Spin, once the Viceroy's daughter has left them, turns out to be a sympathetic listener.

Lear can be quite talkative about his childhood. He describes a great silent dog with a tawny coat and yellow eyes he used to see in a Highgate park. As a small boy he had mistaken it for a lion. Once, this dog had bounded across the lawn towards him, quite silently, taking the whole of his hand into its huge jaws, holding it without biting, leaving the hand coated with its cold and foul-smelling saliva. Lear tells her this in a matter-of-fact voice but Miss Spin says she can imagine the horror and wants to wash her own hands immediately. When the slobber dried it was as if his hand had been coated in resin—'like a clear glove,' he tells her.

'I must be the only woman in Bengal that can't abide dogs.'

She means Englishwoman, notes Lear. He says, 'Fierce dogs I don't like a bit. I'm sure some dogs are nice enough.'

Miss Spin says, 'All dogs will bite.'

'Well, there must be some that won't.'

'My dear Mama had a spaniel called Napier. A soppy old thing. He used to lie beside her when she did her needlepoint. He was always up on the sofa. My father wouldn't allow dogs up on the furniture but Mama would spoil Napier so.'

Lear prepares for a canine anecdote. 'Well,' continues Miss Spin, 'one day Mama couldn't find a crochet hook. We looked everywhere. Old Napier was lying on it, fast asleep on the sofa. Mama tried to pull it out from beneath him without waking him up, d'you see?'

'Oh dear,' says Lear in anticipation.

'And, d'you know, he sprang at her and caught her upper lip in his teeth!'

'Was she badly hurt?'

'Rather. She lost the lip.'

'No!'

'Yes indeed. Napier bit it off and swallowed it!'

'How ghastly...'

'Yes, it was. Well, the surgeon did the best he could for her, but she never looked the same again.'

'And what about Napier?'

'Daddy wanted to shoot him but Mama wouldn't hear of it. He lived till the age of twelve, then a cobra got into his kennel—that was in Jubbulpore.'

'What a dreadful story.'

'Yes well, d'you see, Mr Lear? That's how we lived out here. It won't be at all the same in Eastbourne.'

'I don't think it will. You'll find it intolerably safe.'

'Oh Mr Lear, how can you say that? Just last summer a man tried to kill the poor Queen.'

'That's true but I don't think at Eastbourne. Somebody O'Connor, an Irish hooligan...'

Miss Spin draws herself up: 'We are Irish, Mr Lear.'

'Are you sure?' Lear beams at her. 'I love Ireland. Not the rain, I must say. D'you know Ardee?'

'I have never been to Ireland. All I know is India. But you will find what remains of Castle Spin on the shores of Glendalough...'

Then more consternation. Lear cracks open an egg to release a stinking cloud. Inside the shell is a grey oyster of jelly, sickening to behold.

General Spin shouts across the table, 'What is that fiendish smell?'

Giorgio rushes to Lear's aid, ahead of the dining-room servants.

Giorgio has the rotten egg removed. He cuts Lear a stem of scented blue grapes, no bigger than currants. He pours Lear some water. 'Drink.' He moves the flowers closer to Lear.

The left side of Lear's vision twists away like a rope. He sees Lady Emma coming to the table. 'Oh dear,' she says, 'I am so sorry.'

Miss Spin, concerned, asks, 'Do you think you're going to be sick?'

General Spin, shouting across the room: 'Fellow been sick? Smells worse than that.'

Lear: 'I had better lie down, I think. Giorgio will help me.'

Health all wrong. Had some cold meat and beer in my own rooms, the latter medicinally to set my digestion right and was utterly miserable.

ജ ൽ

Another letter is delivered from Burrapoker Street. It is written in a loose scraggly hand—dashed off, Lear thinks:

Barapukur Rajbari
Burrapoker Street
North Calcutta

29th December, 1873

My Dear Mister Lear,

It was most interesting to meet you at the Palace and we all found you so companionable. I so wish my children had been awake when you were with us because they have listened to so many of your delightful poems. When we are in our country palace, where your painting of the ruins at Filay hangs, we look at it and I tell them that it is painted by the same gentleman who wrote the funny rhymes I read to them. Now they are very eager to meet you. My cousin his Highness the Raja has asked me to write to you, to see if you would be interested in drawing the elephant that is coming—here to the Old Burrapoker Palace! He is the elephant upon whose tusks the celebrated dancer Goki-Bai will perform in the evening. This elephant is called Kalki and he is an exceptionally large bull-elephant belonging to his Highness the King of Oudh, whose court is in Metiabruz near the Botanical Gardens you mentioned visiting, the other side of the river. This Kalki lives most of the time in the King's Menagery (which I visited once, it was rather frightful— there were deep trenches filled with writhing serpents) where

*he is attended by a corps of mahouts. Visitors remark on his
magnitude but also the calm dignity of the beast. The
mahouts only complain that Kalki is greedy. The Raja
thought it might be an unusual opportunity for you to draw
a full-size tusker at close quarters. You could arrive at the
Old Palace in the early afternoon of this Saturday and stay
until the evening finishes. We can give you a room to rest
and change in. If you are interested, my cousin his Highness
says that he would be interested in acquiring a finished
drawing. For this you would receive remuneration beyond the
existent commission. We all hope that you will draw the
elephant for us.*

Yours faithfully/-
Jagadish Sivadeva Dey

'Yours faithfully shillings and nuppence,' says Lear. Elephants
is elephants and here's one indoors.

ဆ ಛ

The next morning Lear is determined to make a better go of
things. In the afternoon they are all going to the Viceroy's
house in Barrackpore, a river journey of twenty miles or so.

Before Christmas, Lear had been discussing photography
with Young Baring. Baring was of the opinion that a
photographic portrait, the sitter at ease with the process,
reveals a profounder truth than any painting. He said he
admired portrait painters and many worked with flair and
insight but felt they must feel their usefulness diminishing.
Lear doubts it. An artist uses judgement. A photograph is just
a record, a reference. He agrees there may be some worth to
photographic portraits—his friend Tennyson is always sitting for
them. Lear has sat himself but he finds the result
disappointing, as ugly as he finds his reflection. Nevertheless,
a good folio of Indian photography would come in useful.

'Oh, Calcutta's packed with photographers,' said Young Baring. 'I'll have a list made for you.'

The list is presented to Lear in the breakfast room. As many of the studios are bunched around Chowringhee and the Esplanade, a thorough trawl looks possible. General Spin nudges Lear with an elbow like a musket barrel. 'A trawl, eh?'

Miss Spin asks, 'Are you having a portrait—what does one say? What's the word? Are you sitting for a photographic portrait, Mr Lear?' Then she says, 'I have a small Christmas present for you.'

It is an embroidered picture, postcard-size, of a bird, rather misshapen with short wings and the large head of a woodpecker or a kingfisher. The bird is covered in tiny iridiscent sequins with a single yellow bead for its eye. It sits on a bough of golden-coloured thread bearing silk leaves and berries that are ruby-glass beads. 'Thank you so much.' Lear asks if Miss Spin made it herself.

She laughs: 'Many years ago, Mr Lear. When I was a girl of twelve. I thought it would appeal to your imagination.'

'Such fine sequins.'

She smiles: 'They're not sequins at all. They're fish-scales.'

'Are they really? How wonderfully queer!'

'Well, we used to live on fish. Didn't we, Daddy? Live on fish!' In a quieter voice, she tells Lear, 'I look at it now and see that it isn't a bird at all but a fish with a beak...'

'I think it's a flying fish...'

'I must say, if you hold it to the sun, it gives a jolly good dazzle still.'

Lear says, 'I shall try it myself. You are so kind to give it to me.'

ဆ ၆၃

The hideous tinted photographs Lear sees at the Bengal Photographic Company's studio in Radhabazar Street (life-size portraits, enlivened with water-colour) are less flattering, altogether less desirable than any work in oil-paint. A row of native dignitaries hangs in the front salon of the establishment. They all stand stiffly, some pop-eyed.

At the John Blees Photographic Warehouse, Lear buys some studies of trees: Buddha's Coconut, the Split Lily Tree, the Indian Beech, the Red Frangipani and the Rusty Shield Tree.

At Bourne and Shepherd he buys some woodburytypes from Cole's *Architecture of Ancient Delhi.*

From De Hone he buys albumen prints of Calcutta street scenes.

From Monsieur Malitte's atelier, he buys studies of tribal Indians, including some formidable Andaman Islanders, negroid, with filed teeth.

The powdery Mrs Mayor (sixty years old with black ringlets and dots of rouge upon her cheeks, whispering in a Yorkshire accent) specialises in harem portraits. These are all dismal, the women looking stolid and respectable—not an appetising harem, Lear remarks to Giorgio, with such beldames on offer. Giorgio is in a snipey mood: 'You are a painter. *Ciò è fotographia...*'

Captain Stretton specialises in marine subjects; Lear admires the pictures but finds the Commodore Trunnion stance idiotic—he buys some fine views of Dalhousie and the surrounding hills.

Nothing worth buying at Mr Humpidge's studio, nor at Mr Lickfold's.

The last photographer on Baring's list is Petrocochino of Corporation Street. Pantoleon Petrocochino is a large Greek gentleman who handles his left wrist with his right hand and rests both on his stomach. He wears a straw-coloured suit with a purple brocade waistcoat like a big cushion, and a black pearl on his necktie. He turns out to have lived in Corfu, though he was born in Chios. 'It is such a small world,' says Lear, beaming at Giorgio.

They are both given cane chairs and glasses of tea. Giorgio is pumped for news of the island; Petrocochino and he have many friends in common. Soon there is laughter, a few manly expressions of grief, as the talk ranges over olive groves and bee-hives. Soon the benevolent photographer is calling Giorgio by his real name, Giorgis. They are smoking cigars that smell of licorice.

Petrocochino is a first-rate photographer. He shows Lear a series concerning a gathering of gosains, dusty men with long hair twisted into ropes, naked apart from their loin-cloths. In one picture, a silver bromide gelatin print with selenium toning, about a hundred gosains sit cross-legged on a section of pavement. Some stare straight ahead, some look at the camera, some turn their backs. 'Where was this?' asks Lear. There is an insolence in the outlandish men that he finds thrilling and threatening. 'Lansdowne Road,' says Petrocochino. He explains that the gosains come through on an annual pilgrimage. Petrocochino tells Lear he is taken with 'the holy fools' as he calls them; he has pictures of gosains from across India.

'Have you travelled widely, Mr Petrocochino?'

'In India, I have.'

Another picture (a citrate print with gold toning) shows two men away from the main group of gosains, sitting at prayer surrounded by a number of small dung-fires. The man on the left's face and neck is covered by a thick veil. His hands are beneath a cloth as well. 'Why is he covered so?' asks Lear. Petrocochino says the man is performing a rite, reciting the sacred words he received at his initiation. Nobody must see his lips, nor must they see his fingers which Petrocochino says are working a rosary. Beside the praying gosains are a pair of tongs, some brass drinking vessels and a short padded crutch. 'And did you find these men agreeable?'

'Not especially. They were preoccupied.'

An albumen print shows another gosain, sitting nonchalantly on a bed of four-inch nails. Despite his relaxed manner, he scowls at the camera. A further pair of pictures are studio portraits of two gosains posing against a backdrop of painted flowers, like Chinese wall-paper. In the first, the older of the two sits on a stool with his hands on his knees and his matted braids skimming the floor while a younger less hirsute gosain (his relatively short braids have been woven into a crown or hat) stands behind massaging his shoulders. In the second studio portrait, the younger man sits cross-legged on the floor while the older man stands to play a flute. The standing man's navel has been painted to resemble an eye. 'They are *Har-Haris*,' says Petrocochino, evidently a connoisseur of holy fools.

'What on earth does that mean?'

'It means they are followers of one god who is both Vishnu and Shiva.'

'They are rather beautiful...'

'That is part of it. The story goes that Shiva asked Vishnu to assume the form of a beautiful woman—this being one of his powers, he did it at the churning of the oceans, I believe—Vishnu did and turned poor Shiva's head. He was beside himself with lust and pursued the woman into the forest. As soon as he grabbed her, she turned back into Vishnu. But Shiva went on hugging Vishnu so hard that they fused into one form...'

Lear buys the gosain pictures, and another of a group of Indians inside an ancient hollow tree. The tree is cruciform; inside its trunk stands a group of six adults and five children, villagers amused and perhaps scared by the photographer. The point of the gathering is presumably to show the size of the dead tree, using human figures for scale. A pair of guards—as if the villagers might bolt—stand on either side of the trunk, one wearing uniform and wielding a lathi, and in a little side chamber formed by roots where the land has slipped to the left of the trunk, is a strange crouching ragged child, darker than the others, with wild hair and a wild hunched posture and flashing eyes and teeth. The presence of this feral-looking creature gives the whole affair a different slant. It seems to be this one's tree. Lear suspects the wild boy lives there.

'This is the stuff!' Lear trembles with pleasure.

'Perhaps you will join me for lunch,' suggests Petrocochino.

'I'm afraid we cannot. I am going on a boat to Barrackpore.'

'When?'

'Oh, we're all leaving for the ghat at three.'

'Is Giorgis invited on this voyage?'

'Only to attend upon me.'

'Then you could spare him, surely?' So it is arranged that Giorgio, instead of accompanying Lear on the boat trip to Barrackpore, should spend the evening with Petrocochino, meeting members of the city's Hellenic fraternity. Lear feels a spell apart will do them both good. When Lear counts them all up, he has acquired eighty-two photographs in three hours.

ಹ ಆ

General Spin, wearing a green silk puggaree and leaning on a cane, is among the columns waiting for a carriage. The death's head beneath the sweeping bulb of the turban makes him look like a pirate chief. Lear greets him and enquires about the rest of the party. 'They have gone on ahead—we're late, don't you see?'

'Are we, sir? I understood three...'

'Not at all.' General Spin is wearing his cold weather mess kit, which is immensely smart: the outer jacket and trousers are dark green with gold lace trim, the waistcoat bright scarlet, the sleeve ornaments are gold embroidered lace with rows of Russian braid arranged in an eye pattern on the top and bottom. There are so many medals hanging from the jacket, Lear cannot count them. Lear, in a pressed linen coat and a round straw hat, feels a bit mere; he says, 'This is too embarrassing. I was sure we were all setting off at three.' The old General takes charge: 'They won't set sail without us. We'll just have to beat through the bazaars.' Lear doesn't like the sound of that. He notices the absence of the Sikh attendants. His concerns are raised higher when a vintage phaeton pulls up, drawn by two black chargers. He descends the wide steps to the gravel with the old man who is festinating already.

'I sent the other carriage back,' explains the General. 'You can't get up any speed in something like that, I said, we'll need a two-seater.' He promptly dispatches the driver and, after being loaded into the phaeton by Government House attendants, takes the whip and the reins himself. The chargers stamp and shuffle.

'Do you know the way, sir?' asks Lear, taking his seat gingerly.

'The way, sir? I was born in Calcutta! We can get there in ten minutes!' shouts General Spin. Lear, pressed beside him, gets the full force of the old soldier's halitosis. He is decaying inside, thinks Lear. This is not wise. 'Sitting tight?' enquires the General with a ghastly skull-smile and before Lear may answer he brings the whip down with a crack. The gates are already open; various guards and soldiers salute them as they pass at a fast trot.

'I say, sir, whoa there...'

Lear's eyes stream and tears are blown from his eyes to his ears, and he can hardly see a thing. The sound is all too vivid: clattering hooves and rattling wheels, shouts from hurtling vehicles, snorts from horses, whipcracks, eldritch shrieks and battlecries from General Spin. His straw hat flies from his head. His thin voice calls, 'Please slow down...'

Lear clings to the carriage as it dives through gaps and spins around corners. They are careering through crowded narrow streets, moving diagonally northwest toward the Strand, travelling at a clip that sends women screaming into doorways. Lear, in a snatched moment of reflection in the terror, suspects the General's appearance as a skeletal Jehu is as terrifying as the speed of the carriage to onlookers. The General screams, 'We're nearly there!' Lear cannot answer, he cannot breathe. The phaeton barrels along the Strand where hundreds of blurred ships shake before Lear's eyes and blurred multitudes of dockers, sailors and flower-sellers part before them like the Red Sea.

'Soft treacle!' shouts General Spin, puzzling Lear who is not in a state for wordplay. The black chargers slow from a canter to a trot and the carriage becomes part of the orderly traffic again. Lear's spectacles hang from one ear. He wipes his face with a spotted handkerchief and rearranges his appearance. General Spin keeps nudging him in the ribs: 'Nothing like a phaeton.'

Lear replies in a tiny voice: 'Nothing, sir.'

When they reach the ghat where the Viceregal Paddle-Steamer is moored, Lear almost throws himself out of the phaeton. There are bearers on hand to catch him. The river heaves with budgerows, boliahs, horse boats, baggage boats, paunchways, cook's boats, morpunkies, hospital and soldier boats. Unwilling cows, goats and sheep all protesting on the ghats; men, women and children, all complexions and costumes and carriages; coops of ducks, geese and guinea-fowl scattered about, hissing and cackling. The red turbans appear.

A regimental silver band strikes up *Heart of Oak*; Lear and General Spin are hustled up the gangplank to a deck strewn with bunting and crowded with men in bright boating jackets and women with hats and parasols, all singing the words by Garrick. There are sandwiches and game patties, chicken's wings and legs and various salvers of merry-thoughts and towering salmagundis of tinned, imported vegetables. Lear eats with determination, he doesn't speak again for ten minutes. There is more music from another deck: patriotic songs and hornpipes. A large rowing boat follows the steamer, laden with supplies and servants. Various narrow country-boats skim beside the paddle-steamer, their crews beguiled by the silver band music.

After an hour, the band is still playing. There is a loud splash and Lear hears screams. 'Man overboard!' Then there is a great commotion with men from the baggage vessel jumping into the river. 'It's Daddy,' says Miss Spin. 'It was *The British Grenadiers* that set him off. He just upped and leapt across the rail. I couldn't stop him.' The old man is pulled from the river. His puggaree has come off and floats downstream like a green swan with its head underwater. The old man is a long wet sack of disconnected yet animated bones. Lydia Spin takes charge. Old General Spin is carried by his Sikhs to a cabin on the lower deck, all the way shouting, '*Sat Sri Akal*!' God is true and timeless.

People have stopped milling about the deck and are sitting now in groups, so Lear can take his sketchbook and crayons and find a place to draw. The trees at the banks of the river are particularly attractive, and the reeds in the water and the lily-pads the size of tin trays. The pencil shakes in Lear's hand, he is still unsettled.

The river takes them past the mills and godowns on the northern edges of Calcutta, gliding into a sparser green and sandy landscape of paddies and brick kilns whose chimneys bring to Lear's mind the pillars of desert fathers. Lear's attention is drawn to three men waist-deep in the river, drawing up a net, ten yards or so from the bank where a priest shouts instructions to them. They lift the net slowly. What they lift from the water, Lear sees, isn't a haul of fish but a single large object that he takes to be a rock. As they lift the rock, Lear sees that it is something softer, a vegetable the size of a small pumpkin or a man's head (for a second he thinks it *is* a man's head, perhaps the General's) with a mottled waxy surface. In the sunlight it splits apart as if cleft and its many petals, translucent, eel-coloured, slimy like carragheen, reach upward like thin tongues. It resembles an internal organ. The priest chants as the men pass the plant carefully one to the other, each rotating it towards the bright sun. There is nobody to explain to Lear what is going on; the steamer moves on until he can no longer see the men or the plant.

The boats arrive at Barrackpore, with a Guard of Honour and yet another band to regale them at the landing stage. The Viceregal party walks ashore ceremoniously, the Viceroy strutting ahead, his beard abristle with jollity. A covered palkigharry, a narrow bed on wheels propelled by two orderlies, is on hand to convey General Spin to his quarters, where an Army Surgeon awaits. It is all splendidly organised.

It is not a big house. Government House is the size of an Italian villa, albeit one with an eight-columned portico and collonaded verandahs; the staterooms enormous, the bedrooms small and few. The staff sleeps in tents. The guests are accommodated in various buildings around the gardens that are the great attraction at Barrackpore. Extending to the river and for some distance along the banks; planted only with lofty or shady trees, no palms to be seen—an eighteenth-century English park like Stourhead or Stowe has been created beside the Hooghly, with a Corinthian temple—even the dust in the afternoon sunlight looks Elysian. There is a menagerie with tall Gothic aviaries and classical pavilions for the beasts. To Lear, an ineffable sadness lies over everything; the tender light sharpens and intensifies the pathos, visible right down to the sweep of branches and the tips of leaves. The park at Barrackpore seems a vain attempt at something unattainable; it all seems temporary, as impermanent as stage property, as if an experiment, bound to fail, is in progress.

The Zoo at Barrackpore holds examples of most the birds and beasts of India.

A bewildered rhinoceros sways and weaves in its enclosure, as if at sea.

'Poor chap has toothache,' explains the Viceroy. 'Isn't that right, Doctor Bruce.'

The Keeper, a ruddy Scot flanked on both sides by native attendants, is brisk in manner. 'We have extracted the tooth, Sir.'

'Then what's wrong with him?' asks Lord Northbrook.

'He has grown timorous, Sir. He no longer trusts human beings. That's as may be. He will have to get used to us. He's not going anywhere.'

'Wouldn't it be kinder to release him?' asks Miss Spin.

'Kindness, Madam, is for lapdogs. The rhinoceros is a savage beast.'

Lear cannot bear to look at the swaying beast, its bewilderment a state beyond pain and fear. For all its classical decorations, the Zoo is a cold, woeful place. Few of the animals will meet the party's gaze but close their eyes or turn their heads. The Bison sinks its horns in sorrow. The Sambar defecates all down its hind-legs and the Hog-Deer stands at the side of its cage trembling with its eyes shut. Doctor Bruce says that the Sloth-Bear sleeps for all but an hour of the day—his ginger moustache quivers with contempt at such idleness—Lear is hardly surprised; he would do the same. Only the Hog-Badger seems cheerful. 'Don't stroke him, please,' says the Keeper, 'he may bite...'

Miss Spin says, 'He looks tame enough...'

Doctor Bruce: 'These animals are not used to affection.'

'That is plain to see,' mutters Lear, quietly so that nobody hears. In a louder voice, he enquires of General Spin's health. Miss Spin says her father's present mood is very much like that of the poor Rhino.

'Does he no longer trust human beings?'

'Oh, he never did.'

A Hoolock Gibbon, black with white eyebrows, spins around a fluted column, performing an act of terrific indecency whilst gesturing toward Lady Howard, the Judge's widow. Doctor Bruce roars at the Hoolock Gibbon with such ferocity that it flops from satyr to rag doll. Doctor Bruce apologises to the women and explains that he is not upbraiding the Gibbon for its disgusting impertinence towards Lady Howard—indeed to him we are just a larger, decently clad variety of Gibbons—but because such vile practice leads Hoolock Gibbons to the same fate as it leads men of weak character—that is insanity. Then they are led into a pavilion where albino specimens are kept, the most alarming being a stripeless Tigress, the colour of old snow, with eyes like blazing pink lamps.

The party, led by the Viceroy, approach Lady Canning's tomb reverently; nobody speaks. The men remove their hats.

The tomb lies on a white marble platform surrounded by an ironwork fence whose pattern is two Cs (Charlotte Canning) intertwined, the whole memorial crowned by a Cross of Saint Andrew for she was born a Stuart.

The Indian attendants stand back respectfully, allowing the Christians to make their obeisances, this is a Holy Tomb. In the background, the lantern-bearers light their lamps, the sun is going down. Darkness spills out from the shadows beneath the trees. Lord Northbrook asks Lear, 'Didn't you know her?'

'It was Elizabeth I knew.'

'Of course you knew my wife.' His voice breaks. 'Why do you speak of Elizabeth now? How can you?'

'Oh no no. I'm afraid I didn't make myself clear. I meant Lady Elizabeth Canning. The wife of Sir Stratford Canning— Ambassador in Constantinople?'

'Oh, that Elizabeth. I say, I'm sorry about that. Still a bit sensitive, don't you know...'

Lear walks alone to the edge of the water. The river lies calm as its colours deepen with the fading light; the reflections of moving lanterns are gold and silver snakes skimming over its surface.

There is a sudden circular break in the surface and a head pops out of the ripples. I have seen these things, thinks Lear, but this time it is a head for it opens its eyes and sees Lear and propels itself in his direction. Lear sees that it is a pale man's head, and as it approaches he sees a strong neck and bony white shoulders.

'It's Mr Lear, isn't it?'

Lear: 'Let me not be mad, not mad, sweet heaven; keep me in temper...'

The voice is English, middle-class: 'Excuse me please. Did I alarm you?' It is a vaguely familiar face—perhaps it is one of the guests; there are so many he doesn't know—a bald head reflecting moonlight. 'I am Slingsby Moore. Do you remember, we met once in Highgate?'

'Oh yes,' says Lear, 'and more than once. The Castle at Richmond as well.'

The bulbous eyes roll. 'Were you there?'

'Don't you remember me?'

Moore dips his head beneath the surface. When he comes up, he says: 'Please do not speak to me of the so-called Daubers. They robbed me. I am entitled to the refund of my subscription.'

'Why don't you come ashore?'

'I am naked. My clothes are on the other side of the river.'

'Have you—you can't have—swum across?' Lear is amazed; the river is surely as wide as the Nile.

'Oh, water is my element,' says Moore. 'I could see the Greek temple from over there. I wanted a closer look.'

'It's the Viceregal Garden. Didn't you know?'

'Nobody told me. I wanted a look, that's all.'

Lear still cannot believe Moore has swum that distance. Moore says, 'I knew you were in Bengal. We both stayed at the same hotel in Taragunje.'

'I stayed after you. How do you know I was there?'

'Oh, I went back again.'

Lear, sounding the older man: 'To pay your bill?'

'I went back there at Christmas. I did pay my bill, as I said I would. It wasn't how it looked, you know. I told Mrs Williams I would be back. She saw me leave. I left some belongings there on that account. I told her I would be back at Christmas...'

'I have some native drawings of yours.'

'Williams told me.'

'But I'm afraid I've sent them on to Italy already.'

'That doesn't matter. What did you make of William Williams?'

'A lonely sickly man. The business won't survive, I'm afraid.'

'You sound sympathetic.'

'Well, I do feel sorry for him.'

'You are right to call that man sickly. A lunatic, I'd say. Dangerous...'

'Dangerous? How do you mean?'

'I believe him capable of barbaric cruelty...'

'Why do you say this? What do you know?'

'I'll say nothing. I have the family with me now. Rescued, so to speak. They are in Chandernagore across the river.'

'All of them?'

'Mother, son, daughter. Not the father, of course...'

'Where is he?'

'He remains at Taragunje.'

Their conversation is interrupted by a long shrill whistle and several guards and lantern-bearers come rushing towards them.

Lear freezes at the riverside. The whole scene is suddenly lain before him: Lear's ordinary frontal vision is changed to spherical vision, he can see all around and above without turning his head—but it is confusing because one's limbs do not follow these spherical directions; best to keep very still.

Lear is ushered back to the party.

The guards point pikestaffs and rifles at Slingsby Moore. He stares blankly at them and slowly submerges. Shouting from the guards. A few splashes. Moore's sleek head sinks beneath the black water like a seal. He is not seen again.

The touch of the Viceroy's hand contracts the sphere into straightforward vision. Lord Northbrook holds Lear by the shoulder. 'Now. This is important, old chap. Who were you talking to? Who was in the river?'

Lear splutters, 'A naked painter.'

'A native painter?'

'A naked artist. Oils and watercolours.'

'Naked? Good heavens. And you know him? Is the man British?'

'I think so. I don't know him well. His name's Slingsby Moore.'

'What was he doing naked in the Hooghly? Where did he swim from?'

'He told me he swam from the other side. Is that possible?'

'For a very strong swimmer. Why did he swim across?'

'To look at the Temple of Fame, he told me.'

'Is he mad? It's just not on. He could have been anyone. There will have to be an investigation. I say, you don't look at all well. I should think it's the sun on the river. Why didn't you bring a hat? I should lie down before dinner.'

The shock of the gallop, the sadness of the Zoo and the oddness of his riverside encounter have left him without appetite for food or company. Dinner is a bore: Lear sits between men who talk nothing but shop. A row at the other table: one lady leaves, all rise in the room. But the noisier women in the row stay on. The fellows near Lear complain of Society. In the cool weather they work off as many as fourteen calls a day in Calcutta. It is what these young men must endure, to reach the Viceroy's private parties.

Then away early, the feebleness of old age. Most exhausting is the tension necessary to stay the same self all the time. There is not one self—there is no self at all—one's current identity is just one's position in the equilibrium.

He sits in the parlour of his little white cottage with a little white pot of Darjeeling tea. He is so exhausted, he sits with the cup and saucer on his knee, rests his head on his left hand and closes his eyes. The day has been packed tight with incident. He is a miracle to himself, soldiering on. Stamp. Stamp. Keep moving, he won't catch you...

Stamp—there at the door is Lydia Spin. 'Mr Lear, the Viceroy insists that you come and watch the entertainment with us.'

'What entertainment?'

Miss Spin says, 'The native conjuror. They say he's frightfully good.'

Lear sits beside her listening to none other than Osman Ali from Williams Hotel, dressed for the occasion in striped pyjamas. Osman Ali is talking in English so rapid as to be unintelligible. Lear picks out 'Lord Tennyson' and 'King Arthur'. Nobody understands his preamble.

Osman Ali puts the end of a roll of tape in his mouth and starts to swallow it. Making exaggerated eating noises, he gets through twenty yards of the tape. Then he reaches into his pyjamas and starts to pull the swallowed tape from his bottom.

There are grunts of disapproval from the audience. Osman Ali holds the tape that seems to pass through his body tightly at either end. He invites Young Baring to hold one end and another man (unknown to Lear) the other.

'Please,' says Osman Ali in strangulated tones. 'Both gentlemen, pull back and forward, please.'

The two men pull the tape back and forth and a considerable length comes out of both orifices and the tape is quite clean and not at all odorous. Even so, several ladies look about to faint. Baring takes the strain, and then the other does, just as if cleaning the barrel of a gun. Then Baring is asked to let go so that the other man may pull all the tape through Osman Ali's body. This he does and as the tape is gathered from the back of Osman Ali's pyjamas, it turns into bunting, a string of brightly coloured Union Jacks. Everybody claps...

Lear crosses his legs and spills the cup of tea (mercifully tepid) into his lap. He was sleeping in his chair. He calls out for Giorgio. How Lear wishes he'd stayed behind with Giorgio—his poor brain is spinning webs, binding unrelated objects together. It's because he is so very tired. A bad night follows.

After breakfast the next morning, the return to Calcutta is by carriage, a straightforward but bumpy journey; Lear, though tired enough, finds it impossible to sleep. If he does drop off, he is likely to jolt forward all of a sudden, losing his spectacles. He is travelling with General Spin (now mobile but quite silent) and Lydia—who makes sure her father is asleep (and snoring) before asking Lear, in a hushed voice: 'Unless one looks at one's reflection, one can't see one's own lips, can one? I mean, not by looking down one's nose.'

Lear tries. 'It depends on the lip, I suppose. I can see my beard, the edge of my moustache...' Lydia tries as well and declares that she cannot even see her own chin, just a poor pearl-button on her blouse, smashed by the thoughtless dhobi.

'But why do you ask?'

'Because Daddy thinks his lips are sewn together. He wrote a little note to me this morning, explaining the position. He must not speak, nor part his jaws in any manner, lest he tear the stitches. I am to remain in attendance.'

'Why are his lips are stitched together? What does he tell you?'

'He has spoken for some time of his alterations. He believes the day will come when he will no longer have a mouth at all but a nasty little orifice cut into his side that I shall have to feed with a spoon. It's all tosh, Mr Lear, but I indulge him. He says it will be just like feeding an infant, except I must feed the wound mashed liver and millet porridge...'

'How long do you think the stitches will hold?'

'Oh, he will yawn or gape or curse before long.' There is a tense excitement in her voice, quiet as it is. Lear peers in Miss Spin's eyes and sees the loneliness of a plain unmarried woman. He knows that loneliness, it infects his own life already; he couldn't carry more. He blows his nose with a linen handkerchief, dyed eau-de-Nil. Poor Lydia sits back, looking large and colourless.

General Spin wakes up, stares about him and curses: 'Buggeration! Demmed inferior suturing, I say. I just blew the stitches away, whistling through me teeth. Use something stronger next time, cat gut or thin wire...'

11

The Word at the Anthrax Club

'He was actually attacked by his own dog, a terrier called Toby, who then stole some sausages. You've never seen such fun! Then his wife asked him to nurse the baby but he threw it out the window! If that wasn't bad enough he knocked her over with his stick. 'Oh my word, he's killed her!' That's what my boy shouted and, do you know, he was right. The old girl didn't get up again. The brute was arrested by the beadle and given over to Jack Ketch, the hangman, for execution. But just as he was about to be hanged, he pulls a clever trick—in fact, tricks Ketch into hanging himself. Just as he was gloating in triumph a crocodile jumped at him. Great heave-ho, back and forth—well, he hanged the croc as well! It was killing, I tell you. Terribly clever...' The older man describes the puppets with such glee; the funniest thing he has seen in ages. He excuses himself, leaving the new member Evans-Sawtell wondering if the Club is all it's cracked up to be. Evans-Sawtell was not at the Christmas Party. The grand saloon of the Anthrax Club at Taragunje, with its portraits of engineers and worthies and its civilised classical architecture, is similar to an equivalent saloon in Lancashire or Yorkshire, save that the scale is much grander, the ceilings higher and the servants here do not wear shoes. All too similar, thinks Evans-Sawtell, is the dismal camaraderie.

The Secretary of the Club, Mr Fisher, stares at the filmy
liquid in his glass and ponders its miraculous power to soothe
torments more psychological than physical. 'Warming up out
there,' he remarks to Evans-Sawtell. The remark echoes about
the lofty walls. He is waiting for the other member to return
before going on with the original topic of conversation, an
incident of pyromania in the vicinity.

Evans-Sawtell raises his glass, 'We're in a bowl, I think. The
air's trapped.'

There is the sound of a lavatory flushing (the club is
plumbed throughout). The puppet-bore joins them; he claps his
hands and the columns ring. 'Warm enough for you, Sir?' Mr
Fisher asks Puppet-Bore. 'This isn't warm,' replies Puppet-Bore.
All jovial fellows, together at the Club. Oh, that persistent echo.

Mr Fisher continues his account (the story that Puppet-
Bore had interrupted): 'Well, Baumer held the maniac at the
kotwali. He was tribal, anyway. After he had burned the hotel,
he was caught trying to ignite the orchard...'

Evans-Sawtell asks, 'A pyromaniac?'

'Not much to look at. Just an elderly Santal, tall and thin,
with a meek look about him.'

'The hotel?' The question resonates.

Puppet-Bore chips in: 'Before your time, Sawtell.'

You old fool, thinks Evans-Sawtell, everything is before my
time; I arrived yesterday.

Mr Fisher says, 'Williams Hotel, near the station. I had to
stay there once or twice. It was run by a Williams and Son.
Chee-chees pretending, as they often do, to be Welsh. Shabby
place. The son was a fool—no favourite with the natives
either—you can be too fluent in their languages, you know.
When the father died, the son couldn't keep the place up.'

'Did it close?'

'It didn't close, but nobody went there. For my part, I
couldn't bear their voices. That minced-up English...'

Puppet-Bore: 'It's the convent schooling, don't you see?
They're always Catholic.'

Puppet-Bore asks Evans-Sawtell if he is Welsh himself. Evans-Sawtell explains that the prefix Evans is in fact an Anglicisation of the French name Yvens, the name of a Huguenot family. He gives this information quickly so that Mr Fisher may continue with the narrative: 'The old man was priapic—syphilitic by the look of him—and the son was mad. Between the two, it was barely welcoming.'

'Were there no women?'

'The old man was a widower. The son had a handsome wife, a silent woman—who they say detested him...'

'Why?'

'Who knows? You know women. It is what the servants said...'

'Was she chee-chee? I mean they usually marry their...'

'Own kind? In fact, Mrs Williams was black.'

'Furthering the divide...'

'But Catholic too. And the two children were bright little things. Horrid voices but bright enough.'

'Oh yes. They're often delightful, aren't they?'

Puppet-Bore chips in again: 'As are the women, Sawtell! Oh yes, yes, yes! In the right surroundings, that is...'

'What happened to her?'

'She ran off with the last guest that ever stayed there. An Englishman. She escaped the flames by a matter of days.'

'And what became...'

'Of the children? They went with her. The Englishman took them to London with him. I expect he's given them a chance in life, Evans-Sawtell. Saved from the Sisters, I'll be bold.'

Evans-Sawtell frowns. 'I mean to say—this Englishman, the hateful wife. Didn't Baumer question them? Wouldn't you think..?'

Mr Fisher rubs his hands, as if washing. 'They were all in Chandernagore at the time. And anyway the mali confessed. He told Baumer that he went from room to room with rags and torbanite oil.'

Evans-Sawtell calls for another gin, then turns to the Secretary: 'Did he mean to kill the chee-chee? Was it outright murder?'

'He said he was burning monkeys...'

'Was the mali quite mad, then?'

'The mali said his master was already dead when he burned the hotel.'

'Is that true? How did he die? Was there a formal autopsy?'

'It was inconclusive. The body was so charred. The former servants said Williams was never well. There were bottles of powerful medicine in his bedroom. He may have poisoned himself with the stuff—his family had left him, after all. Or he may just have taken a turn. They don't know. Anyway, there was nothing to suggest the monkeys...'

'To suggest what?'

'What I mean to say, Mr Evans-Sawtell, is that the body bore scratches, to suggest that the monkeys scrabbled across the chee-chee's body to get at the shutters. That were bolted, of course.'

'What on earth were monkeys doing in his bedroom?'

'The building was full of them. Infested. At least forty were burnt, I heard. Two hundred or more were in the house, it was reckoned.'

'I've seen five hundred in one bungalow on the road up to Ooty,' says Puppet-Bore. He would go on but Evans-Sawtell asks, 'What happened to the maniac?'

'It was decided that the mali wasn't a maniac but an ordinary arsonist and he was sent to Port Blair. The Andamans. Right out of the way.'

Evans-Sawtell drinks the burra peg in one draught. 'I say, what a horrible story.'

Puppet-Bore grins like Punch: 'We are in Bengal, Sawtell. Where lips are black and teeth are red...'

12

_L_ ear is listening, earnestly trying to take in music that he cannot understand. He has never heard anything like it before. The drummer thwacks the drum-skin three times and the beats have an ominous metallic ring to them.

All the objects in the room have lost their heavy restful solidity. Every stick of rosewood furniture is charged. Whether made of wood, stone, marble or any other material, everything in the room has lost its density. Nothing is static, nothing is solid. There is commotion all about Lear. Small coloured-glass bubbles, popping in chromatic sequence: Pop-pop-pop-pop-pop-pop-pop... Red-orange-yellow-green-blue-indigo-violet... Richard-of-York... Lear is invaded by presences. The surface of the floor his rattling body covers is reduced to little more than a point. The impression of the dwarf-servant's presence, the pressure, the encroachment, Lear experiences as a threat, as an attacker attempting to act upon his incapacity. Lear is paralysed—Lear feels watched—Lear feels guilty about something. These three feelings converge.

General Spin is shouting at him: 'I've had my nose cut off. My hands are no use to me and they have altered the shape of my demmed feet. I crawled here on all fours, grinding my limbs into stumps.'

Here is Toru Dutt. She has written a novel in French.

'Is it a novel about India?' asks Lear.

'It is set in France,' she answers and clutches at her heart. 'I am shrinking,' she whispers. 'I lose an inch of height each month. By my twenty-first birthday, I shall be no taller than a candlestick.'

The expansion continues, as if Lear were a violin string being pressed harder, increasingly harder, yet not to the breaking point. He would cry out for mercy, if only there were someone to grant mercy, someone to break the intolerable tension. Which must be broken at all costs.

Pantoleon Petrocochino brings a shahtoosh shawl and a cushion covered with the same brocade as his waistcoat. He speaks calmly, sounding like a doctor or a priest: 'Almost every night I dream I am flying. Last night I was sailing through the air.'

Off he sails, the shawl and cushion with him. Fat lot of help you are, thinks Lear, rocking forward to be sick. Nothing comes—then he feels a buzzing along his spine, a vibration so intense that now he worries he has forgotten what it feels like not to buzz, as if the vibration is the only remaining evidence that he is alive.

The glass bubbles break out of their arrangements to float upwards, loosely, slowly.

William-Williams arrives. He says he has rushed all the way from Taragunje. His hotel, the one with his name upon it, is all ablaze. He has travelled all day and all night and all of today. 'I rode for a while on the back of a goat. Then I was assisted by a gander. Anyway, here I am, with you now and I have this to tell you—you are a good friend, a very good friend...' Then Williams, to comfort his friend, tells him: 'Once I was lifted up and dropped into the chimney of a brick kiln. The chimney turned into a lantern, and myself a burning taper...'

A feeling of expansion, of uncontrollable expansion, which spreads and persists, which tries to swarm, a pullulation, constantly increased by new surges—a state of seething.

Something of huge importance has to be proclaimed, to the entire world, with the utmost urgency. Poor Lear cannot think what it is. He finds himself grasping at thoughts and is caught in a cycle of arising thoughts—thoughts beginning to form, then dissipating, then beginning to form again, over and over. The thoughts are glass bubbles beyond his reach, rising around him like dandelion seeds.

Evocations, fragments of memories, impressions, images, sounds, return in force. The whole of his troubled childhood is told in sensory flashes. Upright cats in suits of clothes, plants, trees, musical instruments...

Lying on the floor, focusing on the visions, he sees them descend towards him. They march about his rattling body like a Lilliputian parade around Gulliver (bound and pegged). Lear feels such affinity towards these tiny memories that he begins to sob. He suddenly feels deathly cold and it is only by managing to summon the idea of warmth that he does not freeze. Warmth represents safety and familiarity. He is lying in Ann's room sobbing, the walls are brown and smeary—gravy, applied with rags—his body curls, he feels as small as a baby—he is experiencing warmth from the idea alone. It is like a great discovery, an act of creation: There! Warmth! And the little parade to prove it.

'*Vattika*,' says the scholar in the green waistcoat. '*Pattika*,' replies the scholar in white pyjamas. Pat a cake, pat a cake—Lear is lifted at the knee and the shoulder from the lozenged floor and lain upon a narrow mattress. A small cushion is placed beneath his head, then his sister Ann is binding his arms to his sides. Ann ties Lear to the little bed using lengths of Union Jack bunting. 'You must try to keep perfectly still, my darling. It will go away but you must keep still.'

'Why do you bind me so tight?'

Green waistcoat: 'We are not binding you, Mr Lear, we are binding Apasmara.' Lear turns his head to see the dwarf-servant hurry past his bed. He's carrying a long curved tusk, the root end as bloody as a drawn tooth. The glass bubbles fizz upwards like a school of sprats.

Two bare-footed men carry the bound Lear through the bazaar on a palki. Lear passes in and out of consciousness. He sees thin dark men throwing flowers at him.

Closing his eyes, Lear pictures a line of men and women, boys and girls, all crossing a flower-strewn valley, gathering where William-Williams is standing on a little wooden platform. He promises them he has a remedy for every ailment. The excited children, the calm satisfied adults raise bell-metal beakers, less to drink than to toast, and Williams sings *Annie Laurie* to them. The people have come for the flowers, bringing bags and baskets and even suitcases to hold them. The children pick for a while but soon grow tired of it and start running about in the long grass, causing birds to break cover and dart protesting upwards into the powder-blue sky, while the grown-ups (the mothers especially) pick steadily on, stooping and snapping interminably the stems that bleed a staining milk on to their fingers. Lear cannot decide where this festival takes place, he rather thinks Corsica.

Lear sees garlands of marigolds and women leaning over balconies to watch him go by. A man with a clown's painted face and a long wire tail runs beside him with prancing steps. If he could move his arm, he would touch the monkey-man, to feel the blue pigment on his fingertips. He closes his eyes again.

The palki arrives at the northern gate of Government House.

Lear opens his eyes—it is marvellous he has not lost his spectacles—to see dear Giorgio, looking repentant, removing armfuls of flowers from the stretcher.

The overwhelming gentleness of sleep. Is there a religion that worships sleep? Lear thinks there ought to be. For an irreligious man, easily bored by Church, on the brink of sleep Lear becomes airily Spiritual, as if dissolving into ectoplasm.

ॐ ॐ

When Lear wakes up, four hours later, he feels remarkably well. He would like to walk. Giorgio suggests they walk within the gardens of Government House; he will bring the folding stool: Lear might sit beneath one of the great trees. The gardens are especially beautiful while the sun is low.

'Let us go,' says Lear, and when they are both outside they stand for a while on the steps. The sky above the Maidan is alive with paper kites, mostly white, some coloured, sweeping around each other, moving in quick combative swoops. Sometimes a kite, its string cut, falls gently to the ground, tilting like a leaf.

A glorious golden light bathes everything. Lady Emma is practising on her cello; the music (an attempt at Haydn) wafts into the garden in long expressive stretches and Lear hears something profound in it that tugs at his heart. Giorgio is hurrying ahead. In the distance there are soldiers, calm and protective. The whole scene reminds Lear of a painting by Claude Lorrain. Then he considers the enormous beauty of the world, and he is so moved that he takes out his linen handkerchief, removes his spectacles and wipes his eye. 'I am not an important person,' he says to himself, 'none of us is. That's the beauty of it. We're figures in a landscape. A small part of the composition.'

ACKNOWLEDGEMENTS

I would like to thank everyone who read the typescript of this novel in its various stages of development: Steve May, Richard Francis, Will Francis, Jayabrato Chatterjee, Katherine Lieban, Kay Schuckhart, Colleen Taylor Sen and Archy Carroll. In India, my biggest thanks go to Prita Maitra, my editor at Tranquebar, and our mutual friend, Soumitra Das, who put us together. Soumitra Das also read over all the Burrapoker Street passages to make sure there were no implausible details and for that I am endlessly grateful. Of course I must thank my family—my wife Emma and my three sons, Llewelyn, Miles and Bartholomew—for travelling with me in India and Bangladesh and for their patience and confidence in me. In the broadest and most general sense I must thank India itself—the best thing that ever happened to me, and the land of my heart...